DEATH

WAITS

IN THE

DARK

DEATH
WAITS
IN THE
DARK

MARK EDWARD LANGLEY

BLACK
STONE
PUBLISHING

Printed in the United States of America

First edition: 2020
ISBN 978-1-5385-0778-0
Fiction / Mystery & Detective / General

1 3 5 7 9 10 8 6 4 2

CIP data for this book is available
from the Library of Congress

Blackstone Publishing
31 Mistletoe Rd.
Ashland, OR 97520

www.BlackstonePublishing.com

For my wife and first critic, Barbara.
And for Chappy.

The strength of the pack is the wolf,
and the strength of the wolf is the pack.

3rd Light Armored Recon
1st Marine Division, USMC

CHAPTER ONE

There was always something he liked about the stillness of a high-desert night, black as pitch and scattered with stars. Its stillness seemed to allow other people's minds to run wild with all sorts of imaginative notions. Either the night was cool and magical, filled with the serenity people dreamed of attaining, or it was inhabited by a litany of creepy-crawlies, ancient ghosts and demons that terrified the mind into a kind of supernatural rigor mortis. But that, he imagined, depended on which godforsaken sandbox you were being forced to play the game of survival in and in what clusterfucked part of the world it was located.

He navigated his way through the sandy terrain's juniper bushes, buckwheat tufts, and uneven footing, creating his own path leading from the vehicle he had tucked safely away in a small wash a few klicks away. Sprouts of Mormon tea and rice grass crunched under his boots as he made his way toward a tall sandstone ledge he had determined would give him the best viewpoint and angle of fire. He climbed over large chunks of rock that remained where they had fallen centuries before, picking his hand- and footholds carefully, as he lurched his way up the craggy wall, all the time trying to keep the battle rattle to a minimum—not that these kids would even know what that was or what it sounded like. Hell, they weren't even old enough to enlist. But they were old enough to be a problem.

When he reached the top of the ledge, he let his biceps carry all of his weight as he lifted himself over. He flung his right leg up in one fluid motion and steadied his boot on the rough sandstone surface. The strength of his leg took him the rest of the way before he crouched and ran quickly across the top of the shelf. As he hit the edge of the incline, he dropped silently and belly crawled the rest of the way, the night vision attached to his helmet doing everything it could to keep his field of vision green.

Sprawling himself out on the sandstone ledge, he thumbed each button to release the legs of the rifle's bipod, listened for the recognizable clicks of their mechanisms, and locked them into place. Reaching up with one hand, he lifted his optics into the upright position and let his eyes adjust to the darkness. He removed his helmet, laid it on the ground to his right, and replaced it with a tan recon ball cap that he pulled from his combat desert jacket. Since leaving the ranks, he had been looking for something that would satisfy his itch for combat by utilizing his training and finely honed skills. After all, he reasoned, what else did he know how to do? He had become a kind of problem solver, an exterminator of unwanted pests. And selling himself to those in need of his services was capitalism at its finest.

Turning the cap's bill to the rear, he shut himself off from the surrounding world, letting his fingers flip up the lens covers on both the objective and ocular ends of the rifle scope. He rested his right cheek against the folding buttstock, its cold familiarity cupping his face like the caressing palm of a woman's gentle hand. His fingers nimbly navigated the dials of the scope, clicking in the windage and elevation. There was no need to utilize the rifle's BDC; a bullet drop compensator wasn't needed to take out two teenagers. This was New Mexico not Afghanistan.

His eye focused quickly as the boys moved with a juvenile purpose around the dancing campfire that silhouetted them behind his crosshairs. Keeping his breathing steady and controlled, he lay silent on the rocky hide of the rise four hundred yards away from them. He raised his head away from the long scope for a moment to watch the yellow flames flicker in the distance halfway up the sandy slope that led to the rock towering over the boys. Their elongated shadows danced up the slope and onto the wall of the formation looming behind his primary and secondary targets. His eyes darted around the blackness that surrounded him, one last operational evaluation of the field of fire. He glanced up to see the sky lit now by only the waning light of a last quarter moon and a smattering of stars that dotted the night sky during the witching hour.

He felt no breeze against his face, smelled no aromas floating on the chilled night air, so there would be no need to consider wind as a factor. But, as always, there was that undeniable smell of sand and rock—a fragrance he knew he could never delete from his olfactory hard drive. It had been formatted long ago along with the sounds of the crowded streets and the stench of outdoor markets and food cooking over an open flame.

He was grateful he hadn't felt the need for the bulky drag bag tactical case for this op. He always preferred to carry his weapon using the sling strap and his hands, even if it did chafe his neck. It held the weapon close to his body and, for him, it simply felt more natural and comforting after all his years in the combat zone.

As his dominant eye rested comfortably again behind the glass of the scope, he began lining up his primary target. He repositioned his legs, then he let the bipod carry the weight of the rifle as he adjusted the weapons elevation turret a few more clicks. He had removed the muzzle break and cranked on the suppressor before he had left; he didn't need a dust signature blowing back in his face, nor did he want the sound of the supersonic round bringing anyone nearby out of a sound sleep, especially whoever lived in the small house he had seen back by the open gate as he had driven up the narrow dirt road. Although, at this distance, he figured the decibel level didn't really matter because it would resemble the soft hum of a kitchen refrigerator. There would be a resulting echo, even from this distance, and would mean he'd have to work quickly. After the first shot, his element of surprise would be eliminated; the next round would have to follow immediately.

He wrapped his right hand snugly around the finger-tooled rubber grip and felt it seal against the dry skin of his palm. Fisting his left hand, he brought it close to his right shoulder and let the bottom of the folding stock rest on it. Instinctively, he slid his index finger gently through the trigger guard and ever so lightly caressed the curvature of its two-stage mechanism. With his eye securely behind the scope, he allowed his breathing to slip into its state of Zen, as he called it. So much so that when his breathing had expelled down to nothingness, his finger felt the click of the first stage of the trigger. His heart began to race as he took another measured breath. Slowly, he let his finger squeeze the second stage of the trigger just as his breath came to an end.

The familiar jolt that rocked his right shoulder and filled his plugged ears with the muffled explosion coincided with the adrenaline pumping through his chest. Instantaneously, the acrid smell of propellant swept through his nostrils. Another aroma he would never forget, but one that satisfied him nonetheless.

He had taken the first of two shots. He watched through the scope as his primary target's head exploded like a ripe watermelon at a target range. Reflexively, his right hand grabbed the bolt knob, jerked it up and back, then rammed it forward in one quick, fluid motion. With another round from the magazine now chambered, he watched his secondary target begin to run as his newly measured breath again came to an end and the second shot took flight.

CHAPTER TWO

The Whitford Funeral Home sat stately on Red Arrow Highway in Farmington, New Mexico. Arthur's first reaction was that it wasn't the type of new conformist brick construction people had grown accustomed to these days, but rather the elevated look of a converted Victorian home, circa 1885, with cream-colored gingerbread that accented well against its mocha exterior paint. Inside, polished walnut pocket doors opened into elegant rooms where back in the day men would have smoked cigars and talked business while women would have been sequestered in a parlor to dish the latest gossip, debate the latest fashions, or even discuss the Statue of Liberty finally arriving from France that June.

The accumulated gathering of somber mourners, Arthur noticed, seemed to have broken off into their respective clusters of family and groups of friends to talk among themselves throughout the main floor. That seemed to be the pattern of most of the wakes Arthur and Sharon had attended over the last ten years, and the funeral home's third reception room, where Sergeant Joshua Derrick's body lay, was no different. Derrick's wife of fifteen years, Kathy, sat in the front row with a few other members of the family, accepting the perfunctory well wishes from the line of people that seemed to stream by at a staggered, never-ending pace.

This is probably the room where the women would have congregated after supper, Arthur reflected, glancing around the room at the tall ceilings and wide baseboards of stained dark wood to match the thick moldings. He let his mind wander because he was trying his level best to think about anything other than the reason he was there. Canned organ music flowed solemnly from the Bose Wave sound system sitting on one of the side tables stationed between two small but tasteful flower arrangements. It had been lowered to a whisper by one of the funeral directors.

Arthur Nakai studied the family members sitting in the front row, sure they were all still trying to comprehend why two weeks ago, on a Sunday afternoon, the man in the coffin had gotten up from the couch during a Diamondback's ball game, went upstairs to his bedroom without uttering a word to anyone, and put a 9 mm Parabellum round through his temple.

He had left no note.

Arthur was sitting in one of the white, straight-backed chairs trying to wrap his head around the fact that Sergeant Derrick had become the latest of twelve brothers of the 6th LAR Wolf Pack to commit suicide in as many years. A transient thought tumbled through his mind about how the older he got, the more mass cards he seemed to collect. But at forty-six years of age, he conceded, his stack would only get thicker with all the friends, relatives, and servicemen he had known. *Pretty soon,* he told himself, *you'll be saying what all the elders say: all my friends are dead. There is no one left from my past. I am alone.*

He shook his mind free of those thoughts and into one of how the sergeant's story had only differed slightly from all the others who had gone before him, but, nonetheless, had ended with the same tragic outcome. He had now officially become just another statistic of the psychological demon known as PTSD, post-traumatic stress disorder. Derrick had locked himself inside his own mind, reliving over and over the sights and sounds of the things that anyone who had ever been in combat never talked about. Arthur sighed heavily. *Some of us never really make it home, because home is still half a world away, filled with firefights, explosions, and death. Because that's the only home that seems to make sense anymore.*

Arthur felt Sharon's hand gently clasp his. He gave her a sideways look and a soft smile before turning his attention to the Marine Corps honor guard standing at attention at either end of the flag-draped mahogany casket. Their dress blue uniforms were well manicured with crisp, clean, razor-sharp lines and decorated with brass buttons polished to perfection. The whites of their peaked dress caps, gloves, and belts stood out like freshly fallen snow against their long-sleeved midnight-blue coats and the red-striped, sky-blue trousers. The glossy black bills of their caps and wet-polished dress shoes gleamed sharply. Arthur's chest filled with pride as he gazed upon their silent, statuesque presence. Behind the casket, the American and Marines Corps flags hung sorrowfully on their stands, weeping the same quiet, unseen tears they had for generations.

The room itself was of average size, but still comfortably held everyone assembled to pay their respects. The hardwood floors were a rich, dark maple accentuated by Southwestern designed area rugs, and they creaked with an elegant hint of age whenever someone walked across the room. White folding chairs were set up in two columns of ten wide and fifteen deep and separated by a center path. Arthur took note that the chairs were quickly being filled with sobbing women and introspective men. Sprays of colorful flowers with cards relaying their sorrow had all been carefully positioned throughout the room on stands and tables, while a large portrait of a younger Sergeant Joshua Derrick in his dress blues stood proudly on a large easel to the left of his casket.

Arthur stared at the portrait for a long moment, remembering the excited kid who had just landed in-country a few months before Arthur's last rotation out of Operation Enduring Freedom. Derrick had enlisted four weeks before 9/11. As he had mentioned in their first conversation after meeting, he "joined during peacetime and came out of basic in wartime." He recounted how his DI had come into the squad bay, told them all to circle up, and removed his cover. The room was silent. Later that day, the company commander had brought in a TV and shown videos of America under attack. Derrick told him of the anger that had filled him that day after witnessing the Twin Towers fall and that in the days afterward all he wanted to do was exact vengeance upon those who were responsible. Arthur remembered seeing in him both the eagerness to fight and the naivety that had convinced him that he was going to win the fight and change the world. *That eagerness always came at a cost*, Arthur reflected. *And all being in-country ever did for anyone was make them hard or make them scared or, like most who came back, make them love it. Love it so much that you would go back in an instant and climb into the uniform that felt as cozy as a pair of pajamas without even a second thought.*

Arthur felt Sharon's hand squeeze his again, and he turned to look at her. He remembered his father telling him when they were discussing his idea of matrimony that life was about choices. And after a while marriage becomes wondering if you made the right choice. As Arthur read the emotion in his wife's eyes, he knew his choice had been the correct one.

"I'm going to go over and talk to Kathy," Sharon said, wiping tears away from her eyes. "Are you coming?"

Arthur shook his head almost imperceptibly. "No, not yet. I can't just yet. Maybe later."

Sharon smiled softly and got up, smoothed out her dark skirt that matched the rest of her somber outfit, and left Arthur to his thoughts.

Arthur half smiled. He was glad that both his mind and soul had been strong enough to tackle what he had seen before Sharon and he had even met. Arthur was of the Towering House clan, born for the Big Medicine People clan, and attributed his sanity to his deeply ingrained spirituality, his nights spent in ceremony, and his resolute quest for harmony. Without that, he surely would have fallen victim to the string of sleepless nights that had plagued so many of his fellow servicemen, over and over in their tormented minds, like scenes from some horrific movie. And not a movie one could simply get up and walk out of. Arthur knew there were things he'd seen and done that would have tormented him every day of his life, much like Sergeant Joshua Derrick had surely endured.

"Fucking sucks, Lieutenant," a familiar voice muttered quietly. Arthur felt a strong hand squeeze his left shoulder. "We just keep burying our guys. Whether we're fighting it on the battlefield or in our minds, in the end we're all just another angel going home."

Corporal John Sykes, who had overseen one of the fire teams within the squad that was part of the platoon Arthur had commanded, was looking down at him, his large frame dressed in somber attire like all the other guests. The years that had passed since their time at Kandahar Airfield had obviously been hard and had managed to add more rugged lines to his already scarred and worn face. The look in Sykes' blue eyes gave Arthur the impression that he was barely hanging on to his sanity and could easily end up becoming the subject of the next wake he would attend. Arthur remembered instantly what had shaken the big man the most—Sykes had blown away an old woman in Musa Qala, Afghanistan, who'd been running toward them with an RPG. He saved his squad, but there was no way of burying that one deep enough. Besides, you can't run away from the things that are in your head.

"It's just Arthur now, John," he replied. "That lieutenant stuff is from another world."

Corporal Sykes bristled. "No, sir. Don't believe that one bit." He paused briefly to look around. "You wanna see the rest of the guys? I just came from the mess hall they've got set up in this place, and they were down there stuffin' their faces."

Arthur nodded and stood. He looked around and quickly located Sharon. She was among the small group of wives that had formed a comfort circle around Kathy Derrick. Knowing he had some time, he wanted a chance to feel Sykes out, see if he needed any help. But he sensed he would have to move slowly with him. "Who's all here?" he said.

Sykes' expression became slightly distant. "Including you, there's only six of us left, sir." He looked at the mahogany, flag-draped coffin. "We're all here."

Arthur nodded. "Lead the way, Corporal."

They moved quietly through from the room where later the sliding pocket doors would close to allow Joshua Derrick's family a few moments to have their own last remaining bit of privacy with him. They crossed the foyer and passed a small but neatly organized cherry desk where a thin, gray-haired woman sat guard in a dark skirt, white blouse, and crisp suit jacket. The hallway behind her was covered in period wallpaper that spoke of a less hectic time, when people weren't so concerned with the talking heads of dysfunction that now inundated the visual airwaves and minds that had not been brainwashed by smartphones. On the other side of the foyer, an ornate staircase rose to a second story where Arthur assumed offices now resided in rooms that had once been bedrooms. They continued quietly, weaving through the friends and relatives of Sergeant Derrick until they reached what had most likely been an expanded servant's quarters and that now had been converted into a room where food could be displayed like a golf course brunch buffet.

Once through the doorway, the room revealed a handful of round tables and padded chairs. A long counter off to the right displayed assorted foods and snacks. Another counter at the far end of the room had been loaded up with black sentinels of brewed coffee, two-liter plastic bottles of various soft drinks, foam plates, and plastic utensils.

"Ten-hut!" Sykes announced.

Arthur recognized the four men in the room right away. Two of the men, seated at one of the tables, quickly jumped to their feet with a crisp salute. The two by the buffet, who had been concentrating on shoveling food onto their foam plates, suddenly spun to face the doorway and did the same. It took only a split second for smiles to brighten their faces and an awkward joy to fill the small room. Hands that had saluted were pushed forward for handshakes before the men returned to either their seats or to raiding the buffet.

James Basher, a cross between Dolph Lundgren and the Incredible Hulk, sat at the table. His nickname, "Bash," came not from his name but from the size of his fists. Dave Lugowsky, who sat next to him, Arthur remembered had earned the nickname "Lugnut" because of his resourcefulness at being able to Frankenstein any truck in the combat zone by utilizing whatever he could scrounge up to armor an add-on kit for a vehicle. The two men waved Arthur toward an empty chair while Sykes went to fill his own plate. Lavar St. James and Mike Dokozinski filled their red Solo cups with pop, plus one for Arthur, and sat at the table. Sykes finished gathering his food and drink, pulled up a chair, and squeezed himself into the group.

"A toast," St. James said, holding up his red plastic cup. "May our brother finally find the peace in death he sure as hell didn't find in life. Till Valhalla!"

The men all tapped cups. "Till Valhalla!"

Arthur took stock of his command, or what was left of it. He studied St. James and Dokozinski—on the surface both appeared unfazed by the trauma of war. St. James' eyes were clear, and he showed no signs of what the shrinks at the VA would call meeting the DSM-5: Diagnostic and Statistical Manual of Mental Disorders. There were six men from his unit dead already whom the VA had failed. Left to fend for themselves, they had taken the only avenue open to them to stop the pain. And he had buried them all.

Dokozinski's blond crew cut looked good on his blocky head. High and tight. And by the look of his body, Arthur could see that Dok had kept up his grueling workout regimen. Bash, on the other hand, was harder to read. There was no giveaway, no clue in his looks or behavior that Arthur could pick up on. Lugnut was another story altogether. There was some kind of vibe that emanated from him like a scattered high-intensity frequency that Arthur just couldn't put a finger on. The skinny kid who had wrangled a .50 caliber machine gun on top of a scout truck in the provinces of Afghanistan hadn't added much weight to his frame since he had been home.

"How you guys holding up?" Arthur asked. "I know it gets tougher … tougher every time one of our own falls." Arthur studied their faces. "We all still carry our demons."

"That's why some of us just say 'fuck it' and blow our

fucking brains out," Sykes said before spitting out his chewing gum into a napkin and drinking again from his red plastic cup. "There's plenty of scars on the inside no one can see."

"Yeah," Dok chimed in, "when you're in the CZ, it's like death is always right next to you, whispering in your ear." Dok took a big gulp from his cup and swallowed hard. "And it's always hard not to listen. You just can't fucking get away from that shit."

"Any of you have luck with the VA?" Arthur said.

They laughed.

"They had me seeing a psychologist *and* a psychiatrist," Sykes replied. "I told them both I didn't want any drugs, that too many guys I knew had a shitload of bad reactions to 'em. They said, 'okay, we understand, no drugs.' Then I had another appointment a few months later, and they handed me a prescription for goddamn pills!"

"What'd they give you?" Dok asked.

Sykes huffed disgustedly. "Trazodone." He shrugged. "I ended up takin' 'em, but all they did was fuck me up worse, so I flushed 'em." He shook his head, thinking back to it. "By then, it was too late. I'd already lost my wife and my kid. I was just in too many dark places for her, I guess. She couldn't take it anymore, so she took my son and left. I got divorce papers served on me a month later."

"That's rough, man," Dok said. "But let me guess: the pills made you feel like shit and the nightmares they were supposed to handle got more vivid?"

Sykes looked from under his brow at him. "How'd you know that?"

Dok nodded. "Happened to me too, bro. The silence will kill you, man. Nothing worse than the silence inside your own head."

Arthur's cell phone suddenly began to vibrate and buzz in his jacket pocket. He apologized for shattering what was turning into a badly needed support group and moved away from the table. Pulling out his phone, he saw the name and tapped Accept. Immediately he heard Margaret Tabaaha's frantic voice filling his ear.

"Both my sons are dead!" she screamed between sobs. "Someone murdered them! Someone has taken them from me!"

CHAPTER THREE

Arthur apologized to his men, promised they would stay in touch, and went back to the reception room where he sought out Sharon before leaving the funeral home to drive out to Flat Iron Rock. She told him not to worry, that she would stay with Kathy Derrick, and after that, if Arthur was going to be too late getting back to pick her up, she would find something else to do in town until he returned.

Slipping on his sunglasses, he shed his dark suit jacket as he walked outside and into the sweltering afternoon heat. He tossed the jacket onto the back seat of the Bronco as he climbed in; the tie soon followed. Sharon had been after him to vacuum the Bronco for months, but he gave little thought to the fact that Ak'is' dog hair covered the cracked vinyl of the back seat. He removed the towel he had draped over the steering wheel to prevent the sun's rays from burning his hands, tossed it on the passenger seat, and started the truck.

Heading west on Highway 64, he followed its gradual turn northward before being caught by the horizontal traffic lights where West Pinon Street turned into West Bitsi Highway by the Speedway gas station. When the green arrow appeared, he made the turn and continued west. The high, blazing sun continued to push its heat through the windshield of the Bronco as Arthur adjusted the air-conditioning to high. He knew the compressor under the hood was fighting a losing battle and had even given a quick thought to stopping for one of those AC-in-a-can jobs every auto parts store now carried, but it was too late for that. Not even the flipped-down visor could abate the sun at its current angle, and he feared it would only get worse until the big orange ball sank completely into the melting horizon.

The drive to Flat Iron Rock from Farmington took less than twenty minutes, enough time for Arthur to let the desperation he had heard in Margaret Tabaaha's voice truly sink in. The thought that she had just lost both of her sons simultaneously was too much for him to even comprehend. He could hear the wrenching of her soul every time he replayed their conversation in his mind.

As he passed the blocky profile of the Northern Edge Navajo Casino on BIA 36 to his left, he could see the image of Flat Iron Rock rising tall against the backdrop of a clear blue sky. *Why would anyone have done such a thing? Who could have had a reason, or thought they had a reason, to kill Tsela and Tahoma Tabaaha?* Arthur remembered that he had been home on leave and had known the boys since the day they were born. He had even taken pictures with his phone and sent them to their father half a world away. In the ways of the *Bilagáana,* he would have been referred to as their godfather. His gut churned slowly as he drove, while his heart ached a pain that he could only imagine was a thousand times worse for his first love.

He was there when their father had been killed in Iraq and felt an obligation to take part in the now eighteen-year-old brothers' lives like a father, to be there for them whenever they needed it. Somewhere in the halls of time, he knew he had failed them. And they were good boys, too, whose maternal clan had been the same as their name—*Tábąąhá*, the Water's Edge People clan. Their paternal clan was the *Tó baazhni'ázhi,* the Two Who Came to the Water clan. He remembered their maternal grandmother had been born for the *Kinyaa'áanii,* the Towering House clan (one of the original four clans and Arthur's own) and that their paternal grandfather had been born for the *Haltsooi,* or the Meadow People clan.

The boys had been a gift to a loving family who had taught them to live in the teachings of the Blessing Way and the Protection Way. Arthur couldn't understand how something like this could have happened. But in today's world, so often it was not what you taught your own children, but what others had taught theirs that would have life-changing effects.

The teens would have had to have been targeted by someone, Arthur had already established in his mind. Of that much he was sure. He had never heard of them getting into trouble at school or in the community. *Was it just some nutcase trying to make a statement?* he wondered. *Or some sick bastard filling his racist need to kill an Indian?* In today's social climate, who the hell could know? He shook his head sadly. *Sometimes*, he admitted to himself, *it really feels like things haven't changed much in the last hundred years.*

Arthur tapped the brakes and suddenly made the left turn onto BIA Route 363. If he had been paying any less attention, he would have missed the handwritten *363* scribbled on the back of the stop sign in a black Sharpie and missed the turn altogether. The Bronco's big tires burped across the steel cattle guard as Arthur glanced at the smattering of rundown trailers and tan NHA housing with their sandy-brown roofs that sat off to his right. Scattered around them were piles of wood and other debris, both working and derelict automobiles, children's toys and a few smaller buildings that sat among the buckwheat plants, Indian rice grass, and scattered junipers.

The short stretch of pavement that lead away from BIA 363 quickly ended beneath taut power lines that stretched between the tall blackish-brown wooden poles that flanked the freshly graded dirt road. Arthur remembered seeing the Navajo Nation DOT graders a while back moving slowly though the landscape, followed by the CAT vibrating rollers that compacted the stone-and-sand surface into a hard-packed road. He watched as the dust filled his rearview mirror before being swept away by the prevailing winds that blew the hot, baking air across the valley.

The view ahead was clear. More buckwheat and junipers were scattered perfectly by the creator's hand and dotted the land from the low, flat mesa on his left and down the slope to his right until his eyes lost sight of it. He took a breath. This was the kind of solitude that made him want to breathe deep, to hold the air satisfyingly in his lungs for a moment before letting it go. He kept his eyes transfixed on the long, hard-packed road ahead.

The graded road made a slight swerve to the left as it moved over a land scattered with small tracts of ragged housing that sprang up at the ends of unmarked spurs that swung off at inter-mittent distances toward them on his right. The road seemed to become packed even harder in some areas and looser in others, forcing the Bronco's wide-lugged tires to dig into the soft-ened sand to move itself along. The road swung left again then straightened out, and Arthur could see Flat Iron Rock clearly silhouetted now against the bright backdrop of a clear sky. He also noticed the flashing lights of Navajo Unit 18 standing guard by the greenish and elongated triangular metal gate covered in the red-and-white reflective tape. The word *SHIPROCK* on the front fender, along with the green-and-yellow swath down the side, made Arthur smile slightly as he pulled up and stopped.

The driver's-side window of Unit 18 rolled down, and Arthur recognized the twenty-seven-year-old behind the wheel.

"What are you doing here, Arthur?" Officer Brandon Descheene called out with a curious stare. He was sitting comfortably inside his air-conditioned unit, the toothpick clinched between his lips moving as he spoke. His short black hair was covered by a white straw cowboy hat that sat above dark sunglasses.

"Margaret Tabaaha called me. Told me to meet her here." Arthur looked ahead and noticed several figures moving in the desert scrub flanking both sides of the dirt road. He turned his attention back to Officer Descheene, who hadn't changed much since Arthur had helped him fill out his application for the department a few years back.

Officer Descheene exited his unit and walked over to the Bronco, glanced toward Flat Iron Rock, then back at Arthur. "Not a good sight, I don't mind telling you. Not good at all."

"What do you mean?"

"Both took head shots, ánaaí." Officer Descheene used the Navajo word for older brother and studied Arthur's eyes as he leaned on the Bronco's door. "Not a good sight."

Arthur nodded and let the news sink in. "You mind letting me through?"

"Not at all. Prepare yourself though," he warned again. "Like I said, not a good sight to see."

Descheene walked to the gate, pulled the T-handle, and swung the long arm of the triangle-shaped blockade open. The metal hinges of the gate cried from its weight in the heat. Arthur waved a "thank you" to Descheene as he held it open for the Bronco. Arthur proceeded up the dirt road and watched the gate close behind him in his mirrors. The road now began to rise slowly and then dip, then rise again and then curve. The Bronco rocked and creaked as its suspension tackled the undulating ground. The truck soon straddled a section where the ground had split, and it rocked more as it climbed the grade upward, past the cast-aside remnants of trash, old tires and the skeletal remains of an office chair that looked out over the small canyon to his right.

Arthur turned off the truck's inadequate air conditioning to save on the gas feeding the 351 Modified powerplant and rolled down the driver and passenger windows, along with the tailgate window, with the touch of three switches. The instant he did, the heat of the 105-degree afternoon swarmed inside the truck like the dry heat of a 400-degree oven after opening the door. Once the displacement of the tepid cabin air had been swallowed up by the August swelter, he rested his left arm on the door edge, searing his forearm on the decorative chrome strip. An expletive left his lips and melted into the hot air, and he quickly brought his arm back inside the Bronco and drove on.

Arthur passed another rusted metal tube fence off to his left where someone could easily turn off and be led farther into the scrubby hills toward whatever homestead or party place might be hiding among the cliffs. Arthur took note of the ragged mattress that was laying on the ground by the gate as he moved toward the Flat Iron, which became more prominent the closer he approached. The giant wedge of sandstone protruded from the land like a monolith, backlit by a cerulean sky and overwhelmed by a blazing sun.

The Bronco's suspension moaned, and the truck listed to one side as it moved up what had become, as of that morning, a heavily trafficked road that led to a murder investigation. Another entrance soon sprang up to Arthur's right. He could see a tan fence made up of six sections of painted steel piping protecting an oil well pumpjack that stood unmoving twenty yards behind it. Arthur pushed the accelerator, and the truck growled up the grade up to where a small mixture of Navajo Nation district vehicles were casting red-and-blue ghosts against the shaded side of Flat Iron Rock. Arthur stopped the Bronco and got out. Slamming the door, he heard that same hollow sound he'd heard for years before stepping toward the revolving lights.

Arthur could see the jacked-up Suburban belonging to Navajo Police Captain Jake Bilagody farther up the hill on the right side of the cretaceous monument, but there was no sign of Bilagody's large frame, nor anyone else Arthur recognized for that matter. Officer Descheene had been the only familiar face. This piece of land, as well as the Fruitland and Kirtland formations that comprised the area, rested just inside Crown-point District 3's border on the Navajo Reservation. Its border butted up against District 2 of Shiprock to the west, which was part of the large Eastern Agency along with Chinle District 5 and Kayenta District 6—all under the command of Captain Jake Bilagody, the commuting captain, as Arthur affection-ately called him since he and the other district commanders were continuing to play musical chairs with the Window Rock district since the resignation of the Navajo Nation police chief

Arthur's eyes squinted momentarily against the sun as he noticed Margaret Tabaaha running toward him. Her long black hair, the hair he remembered so vividly from their youth, shim-mered and billowed as she ran. His heart absorbed the beauty of the woman in the stone-washed jeans and white blouse, who could still motivate his testosterone level to rise exponentially. He forced that thought away quickly.

"Oh God!" she cried with outstretched arms. "They're dead! They're both dead!"

Margaret crashed into his body with a force that rocked him back momentarily and she clung to him tightly. He folded his arms around her as she sobbed uncontrollably into his chest. It was at that moment he noticed Captain Jake

Bilagody, who had emerged from behind his Suburban after making his way back from the fence line that had been strung up to keep drunken partiers from falling off the cliff edge and ending up as food for the canyon's animal population. Bilagody was giving instructions into the shoulder microphone that pigtailed down to his belt radio. Arthur gently moved Margaret from his chest and held her a short distance away, noticing the tracks her tears had left on her face.

"They're dead!" she wailed again. "They're both dead!" She pushed into him again, this time her arms growing tighter around his torso, so much so that it made it difficult for Arthur to breathe. "I have no one now," she sobbed. "Someone took my boys from me! My boys are gone, and I have no one!"

Arthur pushed her away from him again, his thumbs massaging her biceps gently. "What were they doing out here last night?"

"I don't know," Margaret said, calming slightly. "What all boys do at that age? I suppose drink and smoke, maybe play around a little with the *at'éédké*. You remember how it was."

Of course he remembered how it had been. Arthur's mind lapsed quickly back in time to when he and Margaret had slipped away from their friends during the summer of 1989 along the banks of Hunter Wash. The wash had been filled that afternoon by the rains from a high mountain runoff. Once there, they searched for the perfect spot upon which to unfold the soft blanket Margaret had brought. They quickly located a stretch of isolated grasses and spread the blanket out. They had no way of knowing at that time what a warm and fond memory it would become. Looking back, it had been a place to conquer the nervous anxieties of emerging youth while delving into the passions of adolescent love. He remembered the softness of her skin; he remembered the scent of her body; he remembered the taste of her lips, which had been forever

mixed with his because, as a man, you never forget the sensa-
tion of your first kiss. It always seems to linger on the edge
of your memory forever. He also remembered the unbridled
hunger that coursed through his veins as they consummated
their love on that blanket in the tall grasses of that hot afternoon so many years ago.

"Yes, I remember," he said, allowing the curved fingers of
his right hand to gently wipe away a tear tracking down her left
cheek. "Were there any girls here last night?"

She shook her head. "I don't know."

Jake Bilagody had moved closer. Arthur knew he had seen
his small show of affection. "Margaret," Jake said, "I'll have
one of my officers take you home. If we need anything else, or
have any more information, we'll contact you."

Margaret nodded and turned to leave, then turned back, her
damp eyes pleading with Arthur. "Promise me you'll find out
who did this to my boys, Arthur Nakai. You promise me that."

Arthur nodded. "*Ádee hazhdidziih.*" He promised.

Jake guided her to a female officer next to another Nation
SUV and instructed the officer to escort her home. The officer nodded and helped Margaret Tabaaha into the back seat
of Unit 7. Jake turned toward Arthur and wandered back over
slowly, thinking.

Jake said, "What are you doing here?"

Arthur watched the white Explorer drive away with Margaret then gestured after it with his chin. "She called me. I was
at another wake for a member of my military unit when she
called. Another suicide."

Jake shook his head and gave his condolences.

Arthur asked, "What can you tell me about this?"

Jake stood in a classic John Wayne pose with one hand on
the butt of his .40 caliber semiautomatic pistol and the other

hand resting on the black magazine pouches that carried four more clips for the Glock mounted on his hip. "I'm not sure I want to tell you anything," he said.

"What the hell is that supposed to mean?" Arthur said. "After she called me, and I drove all the way out here?" Arthur looked toward the blue-and-red flashing lights on the shaded side of Flat Iron Rock. It seemed as if they had become the spirits of the dead boys, forever trapped in the sandstone like their blood of this now desecrated place. "Look, you know she and I go way back, right?"

"I got that sense when I walked up and saw you touching her face."

"I felt for her loss, that's all," Arthur said. "She's just lost both of her sons. I couldn't just act like we had no history. Besides, I'm their godfather."

"I'm sorry," Jake said, then focused on bringing the conversation back up. "How are you and Sharon doing with the family planning?"

"We're good." Arthur grinned. "She's got us on a schedule."

Jake chuckled. "That's always fun."

Arthur huffed. "Kinda takes all the fun out of it."

"Well, I'm sure you'll get the hang of it. Kids are a blessing from the Creator."

Arthur immediately thought of Jake's son, Nathan. He remembered getting the call at the forward operating base in Kabul. He had been taken out by an IED on convoy. The rest of the team in the Hummer had survived with burns and broken bones, but Nathan had taken the brunt of the explosion as the truck had rolled over it.

Jake inhaled deeply and let it out through his nose. "Where's the boys' father? He needs to be informed about what happened."

"Dead," Arthur replied. "Five years after the boys were born. Iraq."

Jake nodded and looked around at the area. Sweat ran down the back of his short-sleeved uniform shirt and built up in the thick hair on the top of his head underneath his brown Smokey the Bear hat. He studied the cliffs across the canyon and the ones below Camel Rock off in the distance.

"When I was a boy," Jake said, "my grandfather told me stories about those cliffs over there. About how our people used to perform the eagle-catching-way ceremonies in those crevices. This was a sacred place." The big man shook his head. "Now all these cliffs are used for is for our people to drink and forget their lives."

Arthur looked up. "That's a pretty regular thing here then?

"Oh, yeah," Jake said regrettably, looking back at Arthur. "This whole area up here is made up of the teenagers and the forty-year-olds, and every age in between. Hell, we've even had people call in sayin' someone got so drunk up here they ended up falling off the cliff." Jake huffed. "Some of our people are very lost, Arthur. After they tie one on out here, they should have a sweat and clean themselves off." He directed Arthur's attention to the wire fencing running down the slope from Flat Iron near the edge of the cliff. "That's why that's here. But still, sometimes it doesn't do any good." Jake nodded toward the area where the bodies of Tsela and Tahoma Tabaaha had been found. "Looks like the boys were tossing back a few cold ones when they were murdered."

Arthur looked around at the whole tragic mess. "Margaret asked me to help, Jake. You have to let me see if I can."

Jake looked at Arthur wryly. "Since this was a murder in Indian Country, you know I'll have to notify Agent Thorne at the FBI."

Arthur grinned. "You ever noticed how much Washington loves their acronyms? The FBI is working with the BIA-OJS, with internal assistance from the ICCU, but related to the DOJ or DOD type crap."

Jake belched a laugh. "Bureaucratical bullshit! Speaking of which—when are you going to apply for that PI license?"

"I haven't given it much thought."

"Why not? I think it could be beneficial if you're going to keep getting involved in matters you really have no legal right being involved in."

Arthur thought for a moment. "You mean I've been lucky so far, and I'm going to need to CYA?"

Jake nodded affirmatively. "Exactly. Cover your ass, my friend."

"Hey, it's not that I'm planning on doing this sort of thing for a living, you know? I already have the outfitting business."

Jake said, "Look, all I'm telling you is that word is getting out around the rez that you're someone who gets things done, someone our people can count on when the regular channels become useless. You saving Sharon spoke volumes, Arthur. Our people respect that. They trust you."

Arthur looked at the big Navajo cop with a thoughtful gaze. "I left that kind of work behind years ago. I'll think about it, but for now ..."

"That's all I ask," Jake said with a small grin.

Arthur looked around and noticed several officers scattered about, walking with purpose through the junipers and sparse brush of the San Juan valley. "What's with all the extra help walking around?"

"I had to call in a favor from the San Juan County Sheriff's office. They sent over some people from the Farmington and Kirtland substations to help us look for any signs of the shooter, any evidence that might have been left behind."

"Way out there?"

"This wasn't a close-range killing," Jake told him. "And it's the worst of its kind that I've seen in a decade." Jake removed his hat, pulled a handkerchief from his left hip pocket and dragged it over his head, then wiped his sweatband before sticking the hat back on his head and pocketing the kerchief. "Let's take a walk." Jake motioned with a hand in the direction of two blue tarps that looked to be separated by around fifty feet of sloping ground in front of them. "We got the FDMI for San Juan County on the phone right after I contacted the FBI."

Arthur remembered from his days working with Homeland Security in the Shadow Wolves tactical patrol unit that any time there was a sudden or violent death in the state, a certified field deputy medical investigator would have to be notified. The OMI office was run out of the University of New Mexico's School of Medicine. The whole thing, he recalled, operated out of the university's Health Sciences Center in Albuquerque.

The two men passed a small crowd of officers performing their assigned duties to where the FDMI was squatting, dictating her observations into a small digital recorder, being sure to keep herself out of the line of sight of the photographer taking crime scene photographs to document the carnage before the FBI started stepping all over everything.

Arthur couldn't tell how old or tall she was because she was hunched over, focusing on one of the blue tarps covering one of the boys' bodies. Arthur also couldn't recognize which of the boys it was because she was blocking his view, but he could see her gray pantsuit and black shoes clear enough. *At least she wore flats and not heels on this ground*, he thought, laughing to himself that Sharon's female knowledge was somehow seeping into his male vocabulary. Her blond hair was being tossed by the wind that stirred up tiny dust plumes around the Flat Iron. The tarp had been weighted down with heavy stones gathered from nearby to protect the body. She was holding up one corner of the tarp with a latex-gloved hand and fighting it from flapping in the wind.

Arthur looked at Jake. "Must be pretty bad. How much did Margaret see?"

Jake shook his head, remembering the horrific sight he had witnessed through his Ray Bans. "None of it. I wanted her to remember her boys the way they were." He breathed a heavy sigh again. "It's gonna be a closed casket for both of them."

Jake pointed across a circle of rocks Tsela and Tahoma must have used as a firepit, past the carelessly scattered empty beer cans—some crushed and some not—laying on the ground, to another blue poly tarp being held down by more rocks farther up the slope at the western edge of Flat Iron. "Tahoma tried to get away. You can see where his footprints run from here up the hill toward the rock. He took one in the back of the head. Tsela's was in the face."

Arthur cringed, then remarked, "Looks like Tahoma was trying to get behind the rock to shield himself from the shooter."

"Someone took them out quick," a female voice said. "Two single gunshot wounds to the head. Best I can do right now on the time of death is between ten p.m. and one a.m., based on what I'm seeing here. Which isn't very accurate because of this goddamn heat." She wiped her forehead with the back of a gloved hand. "I've lived here for seven years already and still can't get used to this fucking oven in the summer."

Arthur and Jake both turned their heads from the second blue tarp and were met by the green eyes of the field deputy medical investigator. She stood about five eleven and looked like someone who worked out. Arthur could always tell the type. Intelligent women always had confidence and didn't care whom they made uncomfortable. He also decided the blond hair came from a bottle. He felt proud of himself. Despite what Sharon often said, he could be quite observant.

The blond sized up Arthur and smiled.

"Seven years, huh?" Arthur said. "Where from?"

"Chicago," the young woman said. "Thought by coming out here I'd get away from all the snow and the senseless killings. Guess I got half of that wish—the winters are pretty mild."

"Arthur, this is Delores Mendoza," Jake said. "Delores, this is Arthur Nakai. He's here at the request of the boys' mother."

"I'd offer a handshake, but …" She held up her blood-smeared latex fingers. "Whoever took these shots was a professional. My guess is a high-powered rifle." She looked around at the surrounding area, her blond hair still following the wind. "Probably a .300 or .338 Lapua round. We'll know more if your men can find me a shell casing the size of my finger, but that's what the slug we found in the sandstone indicates."

"How can you be so sure?" Jake asked.

"You've seen the bodies, Captain," Mendoza said. "What else do you think could have done that kind of damage from a distance?" She glanced around the crime scene, marked off by yellow tape that had been tied off or wrapped around the buckwheat and junipers. "No footprints means the killer wasn't standing anywhere near this area when he took the shots." She looked over her right shoulder and pointed north across the valley. "Shots that most likely came from that direction. Figuring the angle of the bullet that killed boy number one, which we dug out of the lower rock face over there, I would put it probably somewhere out on that rise there."

Arthur and Jake's eyes followed the trajectory from Mendoza's right index finger to an outcropping of rock in the distance.

"That's at least three hundred yards away," Jake remarked.

Delores Mendoza's green eyes were set smartly in a cinnamon

face that wore no makeup, her looks having been artfully crafted by her parents' genes. The beautiful slope of her nose ended above perfectly contoured lips, and her face left Arthur feeling as though he were cheating on Sharon by simply looking at her.

"More like four hundred, Captain. I've seen .338s hit a target over a thousand yards away," Mendoza remarked. "I think it could handle a few hundred."

Arthur sized up the distance. "She's right," he agreed. "From here I'd figure the flight time of the round being about four seconds. You'd better have your men check that outcrop."

Bilagody nodded, keyed the microphone on his left shoulder, and instructed the officers to move toward the outcrop Mendoza's finger had indicated. Mendoza gave Arthur a quick and intentional up-and-down look and smiled again, then glanced over to the other boy's body. "Now, if you'll excuse me, I've got to examine boy number two."

"You know they have names, right?" Arthur said sharply.

Mendoza stopped walking, turned around.

"Tsela and Tahoma Tabaaha," Arthur added, "if you're interested."

"I meant no disrespect, Mr. Nakai," Mendoza responded. "I do apologize." Her smile turned less bright as she continued her walk up the slope to the second blue plastic tarp.

Jake leaned in close to Arthur after Delores Mendoza had moved out of earshot. "You think the carpet matches the drapes?"

Arthur turned his head and stared at Jake with a screwed-up face. "You didn't just ask me that, did you?"

"What?"

Arthur continued to stare. "You wouldn't know what to do with it if you had it."

Jake's radio crackled. "Captain, we've found something. You'd better have a look."

"Ten-four," Jake said.

Arthur remembered Jake telling him how much he hated saying that phrase, that it always made him feel like he was on an episode of some seventies cop show.

Jake looked at Arthur. "I suppose you wanna come too?"

"Might as well," Arthur shrugged, "before Thorne gets here and runs my ass off."

It took about ten minutes for the two men to make their way down the road and navigate the harsh topography before reaching the outcropping of rock Mendoza had pointed to. Climbing up the ten feet of rock face left dark patches of sweat under their armpits as a result of the unforgiving dry heat. The county sheriff's officer who had radioed was waiting on top of the rise and grabbed their hands to help pull them up, making sure to keep them from stepping on any of the evidence he had located. The officer waved a hand around.

"Looks like the killer was lying here." He pointed to an almost imperceptible imprint of a prone body, barely visible in the loose dirt at their feet. "You can see where his boots laid here and where it looks like he set up his weapon."

Arthur's eyes scanned the area. The county officer had been correct in his assessment. The lack of any real wind in the hours after the shooting, coupled with the fact that it had not rained in six days, had done much to preserve the image where the shooter had laid. The visible sign he picked up had been smeared, which made it harder to cut—to search the land for clues—but Arthur could make out that the figure in the sand stood at least six feet tall and, judging by the size-eleven boot print which had been resting on its side, a man. Mendoza was right. This was definitely where the shots had come from. And Arthur hadn't seen this kind of sign since Operation Enduring Freedom.

Jake thanked the officer, told him to round up some crime scene tape, cordon off the area, and radio for the photographer. After the officer had climbed down, Jake grumbled, "Son of a bitch." He looked at Arthur. "What can you make of this?"

"Oh, so you're asking *me* now?"

"Don't give me that shit. You're the professional tracker here." Jake pointed a finger around the general direction of the scene. "Track."

Arthur began moving carefully, his steps calculated and purposeful. Staying mainly on the sandstone, he circled the hide, if he could call it that. Any way you cut it, Arthur was sure they were going to be looking for someone who had been handling a rifle since childhood and had become extremely proficient with it over time. Or possibly someone who had been trained by the government. Arthur squatted down to inspect the boot imprint in the sand just inside the unforgiving sandstone. "Jake, look at this." He pointed out the faint shape with a finger. "Our man was wearing Evo side zip desert boots."

"How the hell can you tell that?" Jake placed his hands on his knees and leaned over to inspect the faint shape.

"See the five/eleven in the tread pattern? That tells you right there." Arthur continued to scan the sand then pointed again. "He probably climbed up here the same way we did. And I'm sure he must have parked somewhere down the road; most likely through that open gate area I saw driving up. But good luck pulling tire tracks with all the traffic that's been through here today. Including mine."

"You sure it's a man?"

"You ever see a woman with size eleven feet?"

Jake didn't respond.

"I'd say we're looking for a male, about six feet tall with

size elevens, who hates Natives for some reason or is simply one of those fucked-up, racist bastards who's either been a hunter all his life or had military training."

Jake stood up slowly and let his worried look register with Arthur. "Hell, that covers a lot of ground."

Arthur stood. "Think of the skill set it takes to pull off a shot like this. That kind of training is something very few people have, let alone to be able to get off two shots in quick succession. And if Mendoza is right about the caliber, our killer was using sniper rounds."

"Shit," Jake said. "That means I'll have to run a check on anyone in San Juan County affiliated with hate groups or extremists or is just plain nuts. The Bilagáana are going to feel like they're being profiled. Then there are those assholes calling themselves the 'Desert Patriots.'" Jake shook his head. "They've been causing trouble again throughout the Checkerboard because now they've become some kind of Blackwater clone called Patriot Security, running security for some of the oil companies fracking down 550 somewhere. There's even been talk of their possible involvement in hassling Natives recently, but you didn't hear that from me."

"I used to have to deal with them when I was on the border," Arthur said. "Back then, they were just a self-proclaimed militia hanging out on the border at night trying to stop illegals from crossing over." Arthur huffed. "We had to kick their asses out because all they were allowed to do was watch and report, like the rest of the folks down there were doing, but those idiots tried to actually engage the coyotes leading undocumented immigrants across or moving drugs."

The photographer climbed up the outcropping and went to work. Arthur continued cutting sign as Jake worked with the photographer and pointed out the areas he wanted photographed.

The sheriff's deputy returned with a roll of yellow tape and began circling off the area below.

Arthur moved back to the edge of the rocky raise where the two men had climbed up and squatted down. His eyes narrowed, partially due to the blazing sun but also to allow himself to focus on the craggy edge where the waters of more than a thousand rains had cut both shallow and deep crevices into his beloved *Dinétah*. He scanned the rough and textured earth where it mixed with scattered small clumps of grasses and bony fingers of roots until something caught his eye and he focused in. He got down on all fours and peered further over the edge of the rise.

"Jake!" he called out. "You wouldn't happen to have an evidence bag on you, would you?"

Bilagody was beside Arthur in a few strides. "No. You find something?"

"Possibly." He craned his neck back to look at Jake. "Get someone with a bag over here."

Jake pushed a button on his shoulder mic and gave the order. "What did you find?"

Arthur leaned down farther, not enough to lose his balance, but just far enough to get a clearer look. "Looks like a gum wrapper."

"A gum wrapper?" Jake said, perplexed. "Looks like all you found was a piece of trash."

Arthur slowly shook his head. "I don't think so. Looks too new. Colors are still bright and not faded like they would be if it were old. And it hasn't been rained on. You can thank the Creator for the streak of drought this past week."

Below Arthur, Officer Tamara Dan trotted up to the base of the rise with a plastic bag in a clenched hand and started to climb.

"Take it slow, Dan!" Jake's voice billowed like Moses back from the mountaintop.

She nodded and proceeded carefully. Arthur dropped to his belly and reached down to meet her halfway. Snatching the plastic bag from her hand, he continued to lay flat as he inverted the bag and inserted his right hand. Cautiously, he reached down and trapped the crumpled gum wrapper. Once he had taken possession of it, he caged it loosely in his semi-closed baggy hand and rolled over onto his back. He extended his left arm and Jake's big bear claw grabbed it and jerked him to his feet.

Arthur held the bagged wrapper for both of them to study. "You think you can get a print off this?"

Jake took the bag and held it closer. "Maybe," he said. "Not sure if carbon powder and a brush'll work though, so don't get your hopes up. If we get anything to show, I'll let you know." He looked at Arthur. "Getting prints off paper can be done, but if this does belong to our killer, we might have an even harder time getting anything off because of the heat."

"Right," Arthur remembered, "because what the finger leaves behind is made up of water, amino acids, and, ah … damn, I can't think of it."

"Lipids," Jake said.

"Right!"

Jake used one finger to push up the front of his hat a few inches. "Being out here in 100-degree-plus temperatures might make the print pliable or even dry it out. And then there's possible dust or pollens to figure in." Jake held the crumpled wrapper softly with his fingers. "At least it's in kind of a ball. Perhaps it was in the killer's pocket and something caused it to fall out when he was lying here setting up?"

"Then he wouldn't have noticed it was missing," Arthur said. "It falls out up there where he lay because he reached in a pocket for something and whatever breeze there was last night blew it back here and off the rise."

"When he was done, he probably did his best to make sure this area looked like he'd never been here," Jake observed. "As best he could in the dark, anyway. Then he cleaned up after himself but managed to miss this." Jake looked back at Flat Iron Rock in the distance. "This may be all we've got to go on because I don't think Mendoza is going to get her shell casing."

Arthur agreed. "Another reason I'm thinking he's ex-military. Snipers never leave spent shells. This guy's probably doing his own reloads. But you'll need to check if anyone held any kind of grudge against the Tabaahas for any reason. I doubt it, but you never know. And have your men go door to door back at those NHA houses and trailers I saw driving up—they may have heard or seen something."

"Already on it," Jake said, zipping the plastic bag shut and placing it into his front pants pocket. "Anything *else* you'd like *me* to do?"

"Sure," Arthur said, looking around the area from the top of the sandstone raise down to the ground. "Find the killer before any more Native blood stains the earth. I've already seen enough blood in the sand to last me ten lifetimes."

CHAPTER FOUR

Arthur had driven back to Farmington, picked up Sharon, and they were sitting at one of the small-tiled, square tables clustered around the four-tiered alabaster water fountain of the Si Señor restaurant on East 30th Street. They were enjoying two glasses of cabernet sauvignon and sitting on sky-blue wooden chairs painted with bright-yellow sun faces on the back of each.

"Have you heard anything about the Desert Patriots recently?"

"I can check with Jacob Reins tomorrow," Sharon said. "He would know. He's the one following the C and Cs."

Arthur looked puzzled. "C and Cs?"

Sharon chuckled. "Crimes and Crazies."

Arthur grinned as he worked his way through his La Plata Combination, alternating between the taco, the cheese enchilada, the tamale, and the rice and beans with the green chile and meat.

Sharon said, "So how's Margaret doing?"

"Lost," Arthur said. "Her whole world is gone now. She feels like she has nothing left."

"Do the police think the Patriots have something to do with the boys' deaths?"

Arthur scooped some refried beans onto his fork and dipped them into his Spanish rice. "I don't know. Anything's possible. Jake says they've been causing some trouble in the Checkerboard. They've even been implicated in a man's disappearance."

"Whose disappearance?" Sharon asked.

"Is that question coming from my wife or the reporter who inhabits her delicious body?"

Sharon gave an impish grin. "Both." She picked at her grilled chicken breast with Cajun seasoning with her knife and fork.

"I don't know," Arthur told her. "He wouldn't tell me. But his men are going to be checking with everyone living around the Flat Iron to see if they saw or heard anything unusual last night."

"What kind of trouble are they causing?"

Arthur took a bite of tamale. "You just don't stop, do you?"

Sharon's eyes flashed seductively. "I'm tenacious. I believe you find that trait stimulating during certain activities I cannot mention in public."

Arthur smiled broadly. "And what would those be?"

Suddenly, he felt the toes of one of her feet sliding up the inside of his right pant leg. "Tell me what you know, and you'll find out."

"Sorry to disappoint you, my love, but Jake really didn't say. He only mentioned that they've gotten into the security business now. They're calling themselves Patriot Security. I guess they're providing services for some of the oil and gas companies down the 550 corridor."

Sharon pouted playfully, then said, "My friend Rachel over at the *Navajo Times* did a story on the corridor a while back.

Hundreds of needles are already in the ground, and she says that more are coming."

"Needles?"

"Oil and gas wells," Sharon replied. "Do you ever pay attention to anything I say when I'm talking to you?"

Arthur paused in midchew, just like when he was a child and got caught tasting the mutton before it was tabled. "Most of the time ..." he said.

Sharon sighed and feigned disgust. "Listen, the San Juan Basin has been the largest producer of oil and gas since the early twentieth century. There are at least three hundred oil fields with around forty thousand needles sucking our land dry every day."

Arthur listened intently as she continued, laying out all the facts and statistics while they ate. He wasn't sure, but there might be a quiz later.

"Anyway," Sharon went on, "some of our people who own their land signed leasing agreements with the oil and gas companies. But others, those who don't own the land they live on, can't. I've also heard rumors that someone has been pressuring some owners to sell if they don't take the leasing offer given to them. Rachel says that tensions are growing in the Navajo communities because of it, and that chapter houses have become forums for discussion about whether or not it's healthy or safe for our people to even live near these fracking sites."

Arthur took a bite of his taco. "What health issues are being raised?"

Sharon pursed her lips. "Don't talk with your mouth full."

"What am I, five?"

Sharon grinned. "Sometimes."

Sharon added some butter into her mashed potatoes and stirred them with her fork. "It's all about the chemicals being introduced into the soil and how they affect the water table.

During the course of her investigation, she found no evidence that any water samples were taken before drilling began. That means there's no scientific baseline on which to grade any current water samples against." She shook her head. "And the only water samples being collected now are those done by some of the locals. They showed her photos proving how a lot of the plants near the sites are growing smaller than normal. Plus, there are fissures in the ground opening up in some areas that might be the result of the fracking."

Arthur nodded and finished chewing.

Sharon cut and ate some more of her chicken. "Did Margaret tell you why her boys were out there?"

Arthur shook his head. "Probably drinking, like most kids these days." He told her about the empty beer bottles scattered around the scene.

"But you can't buy alcohol on the rez."

"That's right," Arthur said, "but that doesn't mean it isn't there. People are always going to find a way. The area where Tsela and Tahoma were killed is a known place to party."

Sharon said, "Did she mention any girls? Where there's boys, there's always girls. Especially when you're eighteen."

"She couldn't say for sure if any were there, but yeah, I agree, it's a possibility. I couldn't cut any sign because the FDMI for San Juan County was there doing her investigation, and the place was loaded with cops."

Sharon looked surprised. "Delores Mendoza was there?"

Arthur detected a hint of something in her tone, so he merely nodded and ate some more of his enchilada.

Sharon sat back in her chair, a look of entrapment in her eyes. "So what did you think of her? Do you think she's attractive?"

Arthur stopped chewing. Suddenly the restaurant had become very quiet, and he knew he was on dangerous ground, so he hoped his mind would work quickly. "Jake thought so," he blurted out. *Ahhh, sweet deflection.*

"You lie like a rug," Sharon replied, picking up her wine glass. "She's only thirty-two, you know. And that blond hair is a dye-job."

Arthur lifted his wine glass and said, "I hadn't noticed," then took a long sip, washing down the enchilada. "Do I detect a hint of jealousy?"

Sharon drank another sip of wine and held her glass with the fingers of both hands, her elbows resting on the table. "Her tits are fake too," she said glibly.

Arthur sat back in his chair and patted his lips with a napkin, smiling only on the inside. "How do you know her?"

"She was the lead investigator a couple of years ago when those two hikers were murdered around Huerfano Mountain. I ran across her then. She kept some information from me. Information I needed to file my report. Because of that, KZRV got scooped. What can I say? I dislike her. Fake tits and all."

Arthur chuckled. "Well, she seems to know her job. She thinks Tsela and Tahoma were killed with a high-caliber rifle from about four hundred yards. It seemed to me she was right since we found the location where the killer had set up to take his shots." Arthur paused. "I'm going to go back out to Flat Iron in the morning and do some sign cutting when there won't be anyone around. I should be able to tell if someone else was there with the boys before they were killed, provided the scene hasn't been trampled to death."

"How are you going to do that?"

"Trade secret," Arthur said. "Afterward I think I'll head out to Ojo Amarillo and have a talk with Margaret, see how she's holding up and if she knows who the boys hung out with—any girls they may have been close to."

Sharon nodded, then changed the subject. "By the way, I saw you talking to your old team at the wake. How are they doing?"

"You saw me?" Arthur took a bite of taco.

"I walked past the door on my way to the ladies' room and peeked in. I didn't want to disturb you."

Arthur smiled. "Some good, some not so good. But all of them still fighting their own war."

"I'm glad your head was clear when I met you the first time," Sharon said. "I don't know if I could handle the types of things Kathy Derrick was telling us about." Sharon sipped her wine purposefully then cut a piece of chicken breast. "Did you know that he almost killed himself last year?"

"No, I didn't."

"She walked into the garage one day and found him sitting in their car in his dress blues with that same gun to his head." Arthur closed his eyes in disbelief. "She pleaded with him for a good twenty minutes to give her the gun. When he finally did, he started crying. The VA had him on a line of drugs, but she said after a few months he flushed them and disappeared back into his own world again."

"That's why we call the VA 'Candy Land,'" Arthur told her. "Because all anyone there knows how to do is hand out pills like they were candy. That's supposed to be changing." He took another sip of his wine and ate the last of his taco. "I wish there was something I could do."

"I read a story a month or so ago about a group of vets who counted on each other by connecting on Messenger. They would do a group text or sometimes call each other when they needed help coping with a problem." She took another sip of wine. "It seemed to really help. Maybe you could do something like that?"

Arthur shrugged, scooped up the last of his enchilada.

"Sounds like a good idea. If I can stop any more of my guys from ending up like Derrick, I'll do anything."

"What are we going to do about the people you have booked for back country rides this week?" Sharon said. "Do you think Billy can handle it?"

"I have no doubt," Arthur said, finishing the rest of his plate. "He knows what he's doing. I'll make sure he has no truck runs to make, but I think we're good." Then he asked about Kathy Derrick.

Sharon sighed. "She's devastated, of course. Even though she knew this was how it might end, she's still in shock." Sharon glanced absently at the quiet fountain sitting beneath the clouded, azure sky mural. "She feels guilty because she thinks she somehow could have stopped it."

"She couldn't have stopped it," Arthur said quickly. "No one could've. Because no one knows what it's like over there. People here see snippets on TV or read about it in the papers or online and the idiots in Washington talk about it, but no one here at home *really* knows what is going on in the CZ."

"CZ?"

"Combat zone," Arthur explained.

Sharon reached a soft hand across the table and laid it over Arthur's as he continued. "And you know what sucks? You come back home and try to be normal again because everyone expects you to, but you can't. You know why? Because everyone back here is just walking around in their own little world, worrying about shit that doesn't even matter."

"But you came home," Sharon said softly, "and you're all right."

Arthur pursed his lips and shook his head slowly. "I had my own demons long before you came along. I served my country for almost ten years. First in Bosnia, then Serbia, then Afghanistan.

After a while, it felt like we were just fighting over oil and sand … then 9/11 happened. I stayed another year after that. I saw and did things that no one else can understand except another combat vet." He drank a mouthful of wine and swallowed. "And when I got home, I walked with my own ghosts every day."

Sharon had never asked him before, but now, since he was opening up, she decided it was time. "The ghosts of men you killed? How many were there?"

Arthur looked at her across the table. "I stopped counting after my first tour." He swallowed some more wine. "Let's just say, enough."

"I just want to try to understand you better," Sharon whispered.

"But that's just it," Arthur insisted. "You can't. You will never be able to understand unless you had actually been outside the fence."

"Outside the fence?"

"That's someone who's been off the base in a combat situation."

She lowered her face slightly. "I see."

"Before I met you," Arthur said, "I spent a lot of time learning the healing power of the flute, working during the day and spending my nights in ceremony asking the Creator to heal me and reveal my purpose. Once it was revealed, I took it into my heart and let it shape me. But these guys don't have anything like that. Most of them are just trying to keep their heads above water and not drown in a lake of depression."

Sharon shivered briefly because she knew what Arthur was talking about. Because her own demons had been stalking her ever since she had been kidnapped. There were times she could still see the look on Gloria Sanchez's dead face in her nightmares, could still feel the ropes that had bound her and cut into her skin, and could still feel Leonard Kanesewah's hot breath on her neck that night in the snow as he held her against him. In fact, she could still feel the warm liquidity of his blood as it spattered across the side of her face when Abraham Fasthorse's arrow pierced his skull. And what was worse—there were times she could swear she still smelled him all over her.

Arthur noticed Sharon's faraway look. "You okay?"

She startled at the question. "I'm fine."

"You looked like you were off somewhere else just then."

"No, no," she said. "I was listening. Go on."

Arthur looked at her as she sat across the table. He studied the black hair that fell long over her left eye, just enough to bring out her intrigue before trailing off into dancing curls that spilled over the front of her shoulder. He noticed how her dark eyes seemed to reach somewhere deep inside him and touch his soul. And he felt her hand on his too, soft and tender. Of all the things the Creator had blessed him with, she had been his greatest gift.

"War isn't about making you a man," Arthur said. "I know people get that impression. It's about staying alive. And it's about keeping your guys alive." He paused to reflect. "I guess somewhere along the line I failed them, too. I failed my men and I failed Margaret's two boys." Arthur slammed back the last of his wine. "Great dinner conversation, huh? Real romantic."

"It's all right," Sharon said softly. "You should get hold of your guys and set something up. I think it might be good therapy for all of you. That way you can still have each other's six."

Arthur grinned. "Look at you, talkin' all jarhead."

Sharon's smile grew. "I've listened to you a lot over the years." She gently picked up his hand in hers and held it in her palm, rubbing her thumb lightly over the top of it. "And when you see Delores Mendoza again, try not to stare at those fake tits."

CHAPTER FIVE

Arthur's trip to Flat Iron Rock in the early morning hours of the following day revealed exactly what he had expected. The boys, indeed, had not been out there alone in the middle of the night. After scouring the ground where Tsela and Tahoma Tabaaha had been found, Arthur had discovered two sets of smaller footprints in the sand, near the remnants of the beer cans, as he circled out from an area close to the rock that lead down the slope and north toward the hard-packed road. Judging by the size seven or eight they appeared to be, and the fact that one's tread was a herringbone pattern designed for traction with what looked like an arrowhead on the heel and two off-kilter kite-shaped quadrilaterals gracing the ball of the shoe, Arthur figured they were most likely some sort of girl's athletic shoe. The other prints, mixed with the standard-issue police-uniform shoe, were simply that of some ordinary shoe with no special purpose other than to be comfortable. He also noticed that the footprints hadn't seem hurried or frantic, so his presumption was that whoever the girls were, they had left before the shots had been fired. Now he found himself hoping Margaret had been able to keep her grief under control so that she could help him discover whose footprints the seven and eight might be.

* * *

That hope quickly melted away when he arrived at the Tabaaha home. Arthur let himself be led through another one of the nondescript Navajo Housing Authority houses by a woman from his past who seemed to have poured herself into a bottle the night before and never bothered to crawl out.

"You wan' some coffee?" Margaret Tabaaha said in a voice Arthur determined to be a cross between a shattered will and a drunken soul. "Or maybe somethin' a little stronger?"

Margaret guided Arthur to the kitchen of the small, tan NHA house that looked just like all the other small, tan NHA houses in Ojo Amarillo. All had brownish roofs with single carports and concrete driveways and dirt yards. Margaret was dressed in nothing but a gray, oversized T-shirt that she had obviously slept in. The shirt ended just below what Arthur remembered to be two extremely soft but firm buttocks. He watched her dirty, bare feet as they shuffled across the cold tile floor, what remained of her chipped nail polish reflecting the morning sun that managed to seep in through the drawn curtains like moving pieces of shattered glass.

"No, thank you," he replied. "I'm good."

Margaret showed him to one of four wooden chairs stationed around a worn, rectangular pine table. His eyes noticed several nicks and gouges and small carvings of assorted childish designs, most likely made by Tsela and Tahoma when they were young. As Arthur's fingertips traced them, each groove brought with it the sadness of a life never lived and a loss never forgotten. His eyes quickly panned around the contractor-grade cabinetry and laminated countertops, lingered briefly over the brass pendant light dangling above the table where he now sat. "You sure you don' want anything?" she said, wrapping her fingers around the neck of a Jack Daniel's Tennessee Honey bottle that he guessed had been sitting on the tile counter long before he had arrived. She held it up, hoping for his approval. Arthur smiled politely and declined.

Margaret shrugged. "Suit yourself."

She grabbed a glass from the cabinet before sitting down at the table and unscrewing the black cap from the bottle. Arthur watched as she poured more than three fingers into the empty glass. No ice. She looked like she was simply picking up from where she had left off the night before—or earlier that morning. She drank from the glass and looked at him with glazed eyes.

"Don't gimme that look," she said. "My boys are gone. My husband's been gone a long time now." She took a deep breath and downed the rest of the whiskey with one tilt of her head, then set the glass down on the table with a loose fist. "My boys was all I had left. Now I have nothing."

It pained him to do it, but Arthur knew he had to steer the conversation to the boys. "Margaret, have you or the boys ever had any contact with the Desert Patriots?"

Arthur had her dazed attention now. He could see her hollow eyes trying to focus on a thought floating around her muddled brain, doing their best to peer through the golden Jack haze. "You think … you think they killed my boys?"

"I don't think anything just yet," he told her. "I'm just asking questions."

Margret huffed and poured out two more fingers of the whiskey.

"You remember back when we talked about marriage and

kids?" She knocked back the glass again in one fluid motion before placing it down on the table, leaving her hand still wrapped around it. "I shoulda stayed with you," she mumbled as she poured another glass. Arthur watched as the contents of the square bottle continued to diminish. Margaret didn't seem to care. She crossed her legs as a smile of regret flashed across her face, and her eyes looked up at him seductively from under her eyebrows. There was a drunken sparkle to them that led to the long fingers of her free hand curling under the bottom edge of her T-shirt. She began pulling it slowly up her cinnamon legs, revealing more and more as she went, stopping herself just short of revealing anything she would regret later.

Arthur gently pulled the bottle away from her toward him. "Margaret, yesterday you said the boys might have had girls out there with them. Do you know who they could be and where I could find them?"

Margaret held the T-shirt where she had stopped it and licked her lips, as if to capture any of the residual liquor that lingered there. "Jenny somebody and Tiffany somebody." She pulled the bottle back toward her, poured another drink, and waved the glass in the air absently. "They all go to Central High in Kirtland." She toasted with her fresh glass. "Home of the Broncos!"

"Did the boys have cell phones?"

Margaret was drinking the liquor like it were the air she depended on to breathe. And maybe, to her, it was, Arthur supposed.

"Yeah, what kid doesn't these days."

"Then I'm guessing the police have theirs, so do you have yours? I'm sure you are friends with them on Facebook or other apps, right? If we look through their friend lists, maybe you could pick out the girls for me."

Margaret's head wobbled on her shoulders as she glanced

around the kitchen. "It's around here somewhere ..." She stood up, faltered a bit, and regained her balance. As she moved past Arthur, she let her right hip purposefully brush against his right arm and shoulder. He could feel her naked skin beneath the thin, cottony veil of T-shirt, but the meaning she intended was lost in the mixture of day-old perfume and Honey Jack that had already begun evaporating though her pores. And she needed a bath.

Arthur turned and watched as she walked away from him through the doorway of the kitchen into the living room. He continued watching as she raised her arms above her head in a teasing attempt at a morning stretch. She tussled the bush of grayish-black hair that now flowed down the back of the T-shirt to the small of her back and tumbled over what he remembered to be soft shoulders. His eyes were quickly drawn to the bottom of the T-shirt that rose like a theatrical curtain to reveal the still-round cheeks he remembered from their youth. Arthur felt his testosterone level surge as he stared at her smooth and muscular legs, still something to marvel at, before she disappeared around the corner. His heart sank again as he turned his eyes back to the table and the almost-empty whiskey bottle.

He took this moment to remove the empty whiskey glass and three-quarter drained bottle from the equation. He rinsed the glass in the stainless sink and emptied the remainder of the bottle and watched it swirl down the drain. The smell of it bit into his nostrils. He screwed the cap back on and tossed the bottle into her trash can as he watched the water continue to wash the smell of the sweetened whiskey away. Turning off the faucet, he returned to his chair just before Margaret came back into the kitchen. She tossed her cell phone onto the table without saying a word and then fell back into her chair, not even noticing the missing glass and bottle. She seemed trapped once again by her own shattered thoughts.

Arthur picked up her phone, got into its main screen of apps, and tapped the Facebook icon that floated with the others above the thunderbird sand painting Margaret had chosen as her screen's wallpaper. Her page opened up. After getting into her profile, he brought up her friends list and found the boys. He chose Tsela's account first, scrolled down, and got into his friends list.

"Margaret," he said, "can you help me go through these faces until we find Jenny or Tiffany?"

Margaret snapped out of her fog long enough to move her chair closer to him so that her left leg was now resting against his right leg. She leaned in close. As Arthur scrolled through Tsela's six hundred nine friends, he felt Margaret's left hand rest gently on the muscles of his right thigh as he pushed his thumb up the screen. They watched each profile picture scroll by until Margaret's voice stopped his scrolling.

"That's her! That's Tiffany."

Arthur tapped the small picture and opened up Tiffany Maldonado's page. Her profile picture was that of an attractive blond with a vibrant face overshadowed by a larger picture of the Kirtland High School logo, a yellow and purple horse head. Arthur tapped her picture and watched it fill the screen. He held his finger on it until the Save Photo prompt came up, tapped, and saved it. Then he searched the blond's friends until Margaret noticed Jennifer Peshlakai's picture. He went through the same motions with her, then got into Margaret's photos app, hit Select, chose both of the girls' pictures, and sent them to his phone.

When he felt his phone vibrate in his pocket, he asked, "Do you know where either of these girls live?"

"Tiffany lives in Kirtland. By the school somewhere. Jenny lives in Kirtland too, but down by the river."

"Think, Margaret," Arthur prompted. "Did the boys ever go there? Did they ever give you an address? Did you ever pick them up from either of the girls' houses?"

Margaret looked around the kitchen in a lost sort of way. "Where's my bottle? What did you do with my bottle?"

"Nothing," he said. "You drank it all." He held her chin softly in the fingers of his right hand and looked into her distant eyes. "Do you have an address for either one of these girls?"

Margaret's eyelids seemed to be weighing heavily now, and Arthur hoped she would remember something that would give him a direction before she passed out. "Jenny's folks have a piece of shit trailer on 6400, south off 489, I think. Across from some wooden fencing." Margaret's head slowly fell to Arthur's right shoulder, and her eyes sluggishly closed, eyelids made much heavier by the weight of her grief. As she breathed softly, Arthur could smell her warm Honey Jack breath. Without warning, the fingers of her left hand crept gradually up his thigh toward a place they hadn't been in twenty-eight years. He quickly but gently placed his hand on top of hers before it reached its goal.

"I need to go," he said.

Her head rose slowly from his shoulder like it was a large stone, cumbersome and difficult. She turned and gazed at him through damp and teary eyes.

Arthur confirmed, "You said Jenny lives in a trailer, right?"

Margaret shrugged. "Yeah, whatever."

"I promise you I'll find them." A tear trickled down her cheek, and he brushed it away from her face. "I found some tracks out by Flat Iron that could have been the girls. Maybe they saw something that will help find whoever did this."

Margaret's attention span was fading, and quickly. He laid her phone on the table and used his thumbs to wipe away more of the tears that found their way running down her still-beautiful face.

"I promise you," he said. "Ádee hazhdidziih." I promise.

She nodded, managed a painfully numb smile, and sat up

straight with the help of the kitchen table. She self-consciously pulled down the T-shirt as if she were now ashamed for thinking they could relive the past.

"You're a good man, *she'ashkii*."

"And you are a good woman, *she'at'ééd*," he replied. They had not called each other sweetheart since those carefree days many years ago, but it felt good to do so now. "Is there anyone who can stay with you?" Arthur asked. "A friend maybe? Or a neighbor?"

She looked at him through weary eyes and exhaled a heavy breath. "I'll be all right. I'm jus' very tired right now. I should prob'ly go and lay down."

They stood. Arthur let her follow him to the front door and open it. Sniffling, she wiped her watery eyes, stood quickly on her toes, and kissed his mouth, slowly at first, but then with all the passion of their remembered years. Her breasts still seemed rich and full against his chest, and he could feel the lack of a bra beneath the T-shirt and the hardness of her nipples. Their lips lingered, then parted, and she patted his chest regretfully with both hands, remembering.

"I shoulda married you," she confided. "I know that now. But it's too late for shouldas. Like many things in my life, my chance was in the past."

Arthur held her hands gently in his. She was still looking right into his eyes as if she were looking back through the decades to that day by the flowing wash and the tall grass, on the blanket where their passion had taken flight.

"I will find out who did this," Arthur said. "Know that."

"I know." Margaret smiled softly. "I know. But it won't change anything. It won't bring my sons back."

Arthur softly kissed her forehead and left her at the front door watching him walk toward the Bronco. He could still see her as he climbed in and fired it up. As he reached for the open driver's door, he paused. She stood in the doorway, the door closed just enough to leave her face, half of her T-shirted torso and one leg visible. He breathed a heavy sigh and pulled the truck's door shut.

There was that hollow sound again. Or could it be this time it was the sound of his heart echoing the regret of a path not taken? Perhaps he would never know that answer.

The front door of the house closed. He pulled away thinking his next stop would be Kirtland Central High School. However, a glance at his dash clock revealed it was already after three in the afternoon, so the girls were probably on their respective buses heading home. He decided to hunt down the trailer across from the fence instead and hope that Jennifer Peshlakai was already home. He needed a chance to talk to the girls before the police did, if they hadn't already.

Margaret's face, her pain, brought his thoughts back to Sergeant Derrick and what Sharon had mentioned about hooking up with his men somehow through an app. That seemed to be how sentient humans connected anymore. No one actually used their phones for calling someone. However, he'd never been involved in that kind of thing before. Ever since his tours he'd found the fictitious world of online life frivolous and shallow. But he did have all their numbers. Perhaps he could send them all a text saying that if they ever needed to talk to someone—at any time of the day or night—they could contact him? It would be a start.

And today was not any different than back then. All these years later, he still felt responsible for them. Another lifetime ago, being anxious and uncertain got you killed. Today, it was memories. They were *his* men. And that was a duty that never faded.

CHAPTER SIX

"You mentioned in our preliminary phone conversation, Mrs. Nakai," Janet Peterson began, "that you believe you suffer from a form of PTSD." She paused. "Have you been diagnosed by your physician? Did he check for any medical conditions that may be causing your symptoms?"

"No," Sharon said.

"Did he speak with you about any of the signs or symptoms or any of the life events that could possibly have led up to what you perceive to be PTSD?"

"No, not really."

"Then what leads you to believe that you suffer from it?"

Sharon sat on one end of the comfortable couch with her legs close together inside her skirt, hands clasped loosely in her lap. She hadn't gone to the television station as she had led Arthur to believe that morning. Instead, she had taken it off, driven to Four Corners Regional Airport in Farmington, and filed a flight plan for Santa Fe. She reasoned that flying would be faster than driving. By her calculations, it should only take around fifty minutes each way if she used the GPS of the Piper Saratoga, give or take

ble between them where a short pile of *Psychology Today* magazines had been fanned out like a blackjack deck on a Las Vegas gaming table. When her eyes settled back on Janet Peterson, she said, "I fell apart. I didn't go to work. I didn't even go outside. I didn't want to do anything but stay in bed reliving the devastation." Sharon swallowed uneasily and stared at her wedding ring, rubbed it with her left thumb. "That's the only word I can use to describe it—*devastation*."

Janet Peterson crossed her legs and looked at Sharon over the tops of her black-rimmed designer readers. She held the silver stylus horizontally in the fingers of both hands between her tablet and chest. "I can imagine," she said. "And yet you found strength within yourself to go on; you worked through the pain on your own. I admire that. There is a strong woman inside of you, inside all of us, but most of us never bring her into the light." Janet Peterson thought for a moment, placed the stylus in her lap. "You reached deep inside yourself and found her and brought her to the surface." She paused again. Tilted her head slightly. "Did your husband help you during this time of self-imposed incarceration, or did you lash out at him because you perceived him to be a part of the reason you lost your son?"

Janet Peterson watched as Sharon stared at her hands in her lap and sensed there was residual guilt behind the stare.

"I lashed out at him," Sharon said. "I treated him … let's just say if I were him, I would have left me."

Dr. Peterson nodded understandingly. "But he didn't. And would you have also seen a strength in him that you had not seen before?"

"Other men wouldn't have given it a second thought, they'd have just left, but Arthur put up with all my attitudes, my roller-coaster rides of emotions, my derogatory statements

the aid of a tailwind, instead of three hours if she dro
was to keep her trip to herself, this would be safest.

The twenty-minute ride from the Santa Fe Airport to
row of adobe-looking offices on Saint Francis Drive
an easy one in her Lyft driver's environmentally frienc
sedan. During the drive, her mind had spent half the t
ing a watchful eye on the driver with the five o'cloc
the slicked backed hair, and tattooed forearms, and the
spent wading through the river of swift-moving thougl
she could evade this meeting. Twice, Sharon had almost
the driver to turn the car around and head back to the ε
she also knew this added to her anxiety and wouldn
solve anything. She simply had to calm down before b
ered to the office of Janet Peterson a little before h
session. A panic attack wasn't going to do anybody an
that was a fact. So she took a deep breath and kept sil

Sharon picked up the glass of water the doctor
her before beginning their session and took a few sip
ing her thoughts. "I guess because it all started with
our son three years ago." Sharon placed the glass oɪ
table on top of the round sandstone coaster with the
graphic on it. "That was a very bleak time for us."

Janet Peterson nodded sympathetically, but
ing. Sometimes it was better to let a patient elabo
much as they felt comfortable with. It helped ther
safe place in which to share whatever had brought
door. She had always been in the habit of placing 1
her pencil on the bulb of her lower lip as she lis
patients. Today was no different, except for the 1
was using a silver-toned stylus with a chrome pock
black rubber ball tip. "Can you elaborate?"

Sharon's eyes shifted from Janet Peterson t

and demeaning arguments." She chuckled nervously. "I was a real bitch."

Janet Peterson, Sharon observed, was a middle-aged woman with shoulder-length dark hair wearing a dark-blue Hillary Clinton–style pantsuit, currently adjusting her readers as if she were evaluating a fine jewel while she glanced at the square screen of her watch with the pink and sand wristband.

Sharon wondered again if she had made the right choice in therapists despite Janet's degree from the University of Pittsburgh Medical Center, Western Psychiatric Institute and Clinic, and other documentation hanging on her wall proclaiming her memberships in the ISSTD and the ISTSS organizations. After all, Sharon had simply picked out her name during an internet search for "PTSD therapists near me." And after checking out the university online, she discovered it was listed as the top psychiatric graduate program in the nation. Sharon followed Dr. Peterson's hand as it left her glasses and picked the stylus up in her lap and scribbled something on her tablet.

"Mrs. Nakai, I know that what happened to you last year was extremely traumatic. And the fact that you survived with little physical damage doesn't mean you haven't suffered tremendous emotional damage. That, coupled with the loss of your child only a few years earlier, which, I can see, still weighs heavily on your mind, has created an atmosphere within you that struggles constantly with tremendous anxieties and depressions, and possibly manifests itself in fits of helplessness at times."

"What do you mean?" It was a moot question. Sharon knew full well the answer.

Dr. Peterson uncrossed her legs and laid her tablet flat in her lap. "Do you ever visualize your attackers while you're out? Say, out at a store, or in a restaurant, or just out in public in general? Do you think you see their faces then realize they are someone totally unrelated to your kidnapping? Oftentimes people who have experienced such traumatic events have instances where their mind reveals things from their subconscious. A visual ghost, if you will."

Sharon's eyes looked up from under her brow. "Yes, I have. I can be anywhere and see them. Sometimes it seems as though they won't let me alone, so I begin to panic and have to find somewhere to hide." She swallowed. "Their chindi are so relentless. It feels like they're following me from the grave."

"Chindi?"

"In Navajo culture the people believe that the chindi is what a person leaves behind—a spirit or ghost—when he or she expels their final breath. It's everything bad about that person that was not brought into harmony in life."

Dr. Peterson nodded and said, "I see."

"I don't think you do," Sharon said. "The chindi can be evil. You see, when someone dies these spirits will linger around their bodies and their possessions, so those of our culture will often destroy any possessions they had. Nothing is ever handed down to a relative. If someone dies in their home, that home is in some cases deserted and never used again. And we never mention that person's name because traditional Navajos believe that the chindi would hear their name and come to whomever had spoken it. The chindi have even been known to cause sickness or death."

"Is that what you believe?"

Sharon paused, as if unsure of her answer. Then she said, "It's what my ancestors believed. I was next to the body of his woman after Leonard Kanesewah killed her. I touched her. He made me wear her clothes. That's why I can feel her all over me. Sometimes I can even feel her on my skin; I can taste her on my breath. Her chindi is the strongest, and that's why I see her the most. I see him too, but not as often. So yes, it is what I believe."

"Sharon, there is nothing metaphysical about what you are feeling," Dr. Peterson reassured her from her realm of science. "It is perfectly normal for someone to suffer with these ghosts after they have been through something as traumatic as you have. I want you to understand that it is very natural and there is a path we can take to lessen or even eliminate these occurrences." A pregnant pause filled the room. "And there are also several medications—"

"I'm not taking any drugs," Sharon warned her emphatically.

Dr. Peterson nodded and regrouped. "Have you told your husband you have decided to seek consultation?"

Sharon hesitated, turning her gaze to the world outside Janet Peterson's office windows. She watched the trees swaying in the breeze and the traffic that crisscrossed on Saint Francis Drive. She also noticed the similar-looking offices across the street staring back at her like a mirror image and the clouds that seemed to be floating across the sky at a snail's pace as her watch's hands seemed to move even slower. She returned her attention to Dr. Peterson.

"No, I haven't. I didn't want to appear weak in his eyes, I guess." She paused. "I've managed to keep my symptoms hidden from him since the kidnapping. He hasn't seemed to notice my recent focus on work, and I try not to let him witness my moments of anxiety." She sighed. "He's seen and been through so much, having been a Marine and then served as part of Homeland Security. He's just now started opening up to me about it all." She paused again. "I didn't want to worry him."

Sharon watched the dark hair of Janet Peterson remain still as she scribbled more hidden lines on her tablet with the stylus.

"I think we should begin by revisiting the loss of your child; you seem to have some repressed memories and emotions still to deal with. From there we can begin to build a bridge from that event to the event that you faced last year, and finally to where you are today." Janet Peterson looked at her and smiled encouragingly. "Does that sound all right to you?"

Sharon stared blankly and blinked once. Noticeably. *This is it*, she thought. *This is what I've come to face, but can I? Can I really relive every terrifying moment?* She felt the tiny hairs on the back of her neck stand up and her mouth turn dry. She reached out and again grabbed the water glass and drank half of the liquid from it. She felt the quenching relief of the water traveling down her throat, but quickly realized it had no effect on the dryness. She looked at Dr. Peterson and sat the glass back down on the Kokopelli coaster.

"I lost a child," she said. "Stillborn. What else is there to tell?"

Janet Peterson looked somber and said, "A great deal more, I expect, Mrs. Nakai. A great deal. You see, over time we all have a way of pushing episodes of tragedy into a dark closet of our minds. It's called repression. And the only way to deal with repression is to walk into that dark closet and drag it out into the light of understanding."

The remainder of the session went by at a staggeringly slow pace, at least in Sharon's mind. She began by describing the events in the hospital and the stillbirth of their son. She then moved on to the days that turned quickly into two years before she began the slow crawl out of the cocoon she had wrapped herself in. Every thought that flooded back brought with it every emotion that she had experienced at the time. Sharon had taken the liberty of emptying a portion of the Kleenex box the doctor had placed next to the water glass on the coffee table. Throughout the recitation, her eyes kept following the room as it was spinning. She noticed the desk with its contemporary lamp that loomed above its only occupant, an open laptop. No pictures of family or vacations dwelled there, not even a photograph of a dog or cat. Sharon watched Dr. Peterson scribble again as she spoke, all the while keeping a watchful eye on the clock, a fact which did not escape Sharon's reporter's mind and she made note of it in her hard drive. Sharon was about to continue when Janet Peterson interrupted.

"I'm afraid we've gone past our allotted time by a few minutes, Mrs. Nakai. My next patient will be waiting." She checked the calendar on her tablet. "Let's schedule our next session for the same time next Thursday. Would that work for you?"

Sharon emptied the water glass before sitting it back on top of Kokopelli. "I don't think so," she said.

Janet Peterson looked again at her planner. "Then how about next Friday at one thirty?"

Sharon shook her head. "I don't think you understand me." She stood and smoothed out her skirt then picked up her purse. "I'm done. This isn't what I need. I'm sorry to have wasted your time."

Janet Peterson stood and followed Sharon to the office door. "I certainly can't force you to continue, Mrs. Nakai, but I must ask you to reconsider maintaining our sessions. You can hardly judge its effect by one visit. And I can see there are deeper issues we need to delve into."

Sharon opened the door and said, "It's just not for me," and closed the door behind her.

CHAPTER SEVEN

Arthur's cell phone vibrated with a series of long buzzes, wrenching him away from his thoughts as he pulled away from Margaret's house. He regrouped quickly when he saw Sharon's name and photo. He put the phone on speaker and answered, "Chaco Pizza!"

Sharon's laughter on the other end of the phone made him smile. He could see her face in his mind's eye as he began driving toward the trailer home of Jennifer Peshlakai. When she stopped laughing, she reported in. "The Desert Patriots have a compound northwest of Counselor. Jacob was out on location today, so I hit him up when he got back to the station."

"Does he think they could be involved in this?"

"He wouldn't put it past them, but he wasn't going to speculate. However, he did say there was an unsubstantiated report that a Navajo man in his midfifties was beaten up at a gas station north of Counselor by some roughnecks from one of the oil companies last week, and no one has seen the alleged victim since the attack. And no one has shown up at a rez clinic or a hospital either."

"Someone has to be missing him?"

"Of course someone is missing him. Just like there's about a thousand parents still missing the five hundred and twelve girls and women that disappeared off the rez last year. Jacob said there was a missing persons report filed over in Nageezi about a man fitting the description who hasn't come home after a few days," Sharon said, "but the Nation Police don't have any way to connect the two. It's like he just vanished."

"No one just vanishes," Arthur remarked, "unless they want to start a new life or they're dead."

Sharon agreed, then added, "Jacob says the Patriots were hired by NMX as security around a year and a half ago to protect their oil and gas wells, man camps and the current fracking sites they have scattered over a good section of the 550 corridor because of all the resistance from the Water Protectors."

"New Mexico Xploration?" Arthur said.

"That's right. Seems the Patriots claim to be a Blackwater-type security company now, and Jacob's heard of their people already having a few altercations with folks in some of the border towns, but no one there is talking."

"Are they still run by Elias Dayton?"

"How did you know?" Sharon said.

"We met in a past life."

"Okay, well, turns out Jacob did a story on him last year. This Elias Dayton claims to be descended from an American patriot from the Revolutionary War, but that can't be substantiated. They've been working the security angle now for the past five years."

"Text me the location of the compound," Arthur said, "and I'll see what I can get from the man himself."

"What? You can't just show up there and expect to be welcomed in," Sharon warned.

"I know this asshole," Arthur said. "I dealt with him as

a Shadow Wolf." Guiding the Bronco out of the subdivision, Margaret's kiss still lingered in his mind and on his lips. It was a memory that part of him wanted to hold on to, but another part of him told him he had to let go. The past was the past. Never to again be the present. "Hey, I left you two messages. How come you didn't call me back?"

"We had a production meeting this morning," Sharon lied. "The usual boring BS. Add that to the high temperatures causing everyone's brains to explode, and crime is having a field day today." She waited for him to respond. When he didn't, she said, "Will you be ready for tonight, babe?"

"What's tonight?"

"You know?" Sharon's voice had become low and a little muffled as she spoke into her end of the phone. "I bought a kit today. It says I'm ovulating."

"Oh," Arthur said. "Nothing I like better than performing on a schedule."

"You told me it didn't bother you," Sharon said. "Now it does?"

"No, not really," he backtracked, "I just feel a little like a dancing monkey in the circus."

There was a short moment of dead air. "Well, the circus will be in town for about three days, and unless you want the main tent to close up for a month, I suggest you get yourself home tonight and dance for me."

Arthur chose the lesser of two evils. "Well, since you put it that way …" His words trailed off.

"You be careful now," Sharon said and ended the call.

She could be very convincing when she needed to be, Arthur reminded himself, and this had been one of those times. He knew the thought of trying for another child meant everything to her. And the fact that she was so excited about the possibility meant everything to him. But he realized that if it were even possible to get back to the way they were before, it was going to be a long and slow path of compromise and understanding. But it was a path worth walking if their marriage was to survive the tragedies of their past. People were imperfect creatures and marriages were imperfect unions, he mused, and the only happily ever afters were those found in Hallmark movies or romance novels. He grinned to himself. But even that came after many miscommunications and juvenile misjudgments.

Sharon's text came through with the Patriot address. Arthur tucked his phone into his shirt pocket and continued toward Jennifer Peshlakai's trailer off 6400. As he drove, Margaret's face once again appeared in his heart like a lingering emotion. How could the girl who had been so full of promise, he asked himself, the girl he had once loved, become the woman he just saw, a woman left with nothing but the memories of an all-too-short past and a future that no longer existed? Her life had simply ceased working, like a windup clock that ran out of spring tension, with the firing of two rounds from a rifle. Time had literally been stopped by someone she never even knew existed, and who had taken away her entire world. Maybe he could make a call to see if someone from the local chapter house could check in on her from time to time. Someone was always there handling whatever events they were planning. Maybe that would help ease his mind ... and his conscience.

It didn't take long for Arthur to navigate his way out of the subdivision and make the left turn onto North 3005, just past the red roof of the NHA Housing Management office. The NAPI drip-arrogation crops flanked him on either side as he drove back to BIA Route 36. He turned left again and headed toward Nenahnezad, hoping Margaret had been sober enough to know what she was talking about and had not sent him out chasing wild geese.

When he crossed the 6675 bridge that stretched over the shallow brown waters that split around the sandbar in the middle of the San Juan River, he wondered why the thought of Margaret kept tugging on his mind. Was it because a man always carried with him a torch for his first love? For the girl who taught him how to explore the perfection of the female form and learn of its gifts? Or was it because he felt a deepening, gut-wrenching sadness for her? For what she had now become? He pushed the thought from his mind as he drove by a few small shack homes with even smaller sheds behind them and wound his way around to Old Kirtland Highway. He turned right at Golden's Food Store and headed east.

Arthur covered the two miles between Fruitland and Kirtland in roughly five minutes before turning south onto 6400 across from a white aluminum building with corrugated sides wearing a black spray can of graffiti on its front wall. He was wishing his wolf-dog, Ak'is, was with him. At least he would've had someone to talk to while driving. A one-sided conversation was better than none at all, he figured, but the reality was that it was far too hot for Ak'is to be cooped up in the Bronco while he was talking to people and trying to get information. At least, he reflected, talking sounded better than interrogating.

The parched earth that surrounded most of the homes down 6400 was scattered with sparse trees big enough to be called shade trees and were offset by those brandishing a few green lawns. Stacks of piled branches littered the edges of the road around some of the homes as Arthur kept his speed to the prescribed twenty-five mph. He moved slowly down the empty street, past gravel parking areas, chain-link fences, and the scattered small rows of manicured shrubs that did their best to separate those few existing lawns from the street.

The subdivision looked to have been designed to be large and open, and the clear blue sky that hung above it made everything appear that way. He moved past the CenturyLink substation and the Kirtland Vet Clinic with its cinder block walls of pale yellow, toward the river and hopefully Jennifer Peshlakai's trailer. Kids bounced on a trampoline in a backyard to his left, and he waved to them as he passed. He got no response, just stares at what they must have considered to be an unidentified intruding vehicle. Approaching a tall row of trees shading a green lawn guarded by a white plank fence ahead on his left, he noticed the single-wide trailer across from the wooden fence Margaret had mentioned.

The street turned to packed gravel as he looked out to examine the barren land on the corner where the trailer sat. It was a forty-four-foot lime-green Bellavista with wooden lattice over the bay window that someone had added above the covered tongue on the front of the trailer. The aluminum skin of its sides was dented and well-worn from years of bad weather and neglect, and the corner dirt lot seemed strewn with rocks and clusters of small tufts of weeds. A cinder block firepit sat far enough from the trailer to be considered safe and surrounded a captive pile of charred logs that had been allowed to burn out on their own.

The whole lot could have been used for parking since it was devoid of any other usefulness, and the only tree visible stood on the other side of the trailer but offered it no useful shade. Arthur made note of the five windows facing the street and of the two doors, the main one most likely entering into a kitchen seating area while the other probably gave egress to a back bedroom. One of the windows he could see was open because the yellowed lace curtains moved in the hot breeze. The steps leading up to the front door were a mixture of leftover aluminum siding and graying wood, and the Yamaha ATV squatting beside them led Arthur to believe someone was home. No one leaves six to eleven grand standing alone like a bashful boy at a dance without an eye to watch over it.

He took a deep breath and drove the Bronco onto the dirt lot and parked near the ATV. A cloud of dust wafted past him as he got out and closed the door. The door once again made that same reverberating hollow sound that always rang in his ears. The only difference was today it sounded as hollow as Margaret's heart.

Arthur made his way to the rickety steps and rapped his knuckles on the storm door. After thirty seconds, he knocked again. This time more firmly, rattling the aluminum and plexiglass of the door. Another thirty seconds passed before the inside door swung open and a Native woman appeared. Her black hair was tied back into a ponytail due to the heat, as Arthur knew from Sharon's past hairstyles, and she wore a ribbed blue Henley tank top with the first two snaps unsnapped. A pair of white shorts cut short enough to expose the front pockets below the frayed edges led to muscular legs that ran down past where the storm door hid her calves and feet.

"Who are you?" the woman asked.

"Are you Jennifer Peshlakai's mother?"

The woman looked at him suspiciously. "She in trouble again?" Arthur watched her eyes glance up the street. "What's she done now?"

"Do you think I could come in out of the heat?" He wiped his forehead. "And do you suppose I could trouble you for some cold water?"

"You some kinda cop?" the woman said. "Show me a badge."

Arthur put a tentative foot on the bottom of the uneasy steps. The wind had changed direction and brought with it the aroma of shallow, slow-moving river water evaporating over scattered rocks in the hot sun.

Perhaps, Arthur thought, Jake was right about the PI thing. He could have business cards to hand out that would bypass all this wordplay. "Not a cop," he said, "Diné or otherwise. I just need to speak with your daughter. Is she home? I'm hoping she may know something about the two boys that were killed out by Flat Iron Rock."

The woman bristled. "Why would she know about that?"

"Because she was a friend of the boys who were killed. And from what I've been told, she was a rather close friend. I just need to ask her some questions."

"If you're not a cop, what did the boys mean to you?" She looked up the street again.

"Their mother asked me if I would look into it, see if there was anything I could find out." He paused. "I'm hoping your daughter can help me do that."

The woman ran a bruised hand over her forehead and opened the storm door. "C'mon in. But make it quick. My husband will be home soon, and you don't want him finding you here."

"Jealous type?"

She let the storm door rattle shut before pushing the entry door closed. "He's a *acho'*."

Arthur held back a smile. Calling her husband a dick had said it all. As he glanced around the disheveled trailer, he could hear the AC unit on the roof trying its best to make it comfortable during the heat of the day. But, Arthur noted, it also didn't help that the window where he had seen the curtains moving was missing its glass. The rest of the windows were covered in patterned curtains that at one time had the matched the seat cushions of the dinette. Now both looked as worn out as the trailer's shell did.

"Is your daughter here?"

Jennifer Peshlakai's mother pulled a cold bottle of water from the small refrigerator in the tiny kitchenette and handed it to her unexpected guest. Arthur took it and unscrewed the cap.

"No, she's not," she said. "I haven't seen her since I heard the news about the boys."

The fact that it seemed not to bother her gave him pause. "Have you tried calling her?"

"Of course I've tried. Several times." She stepped over to the patterned covered window and peeked out. "It's not like her. She always answers."

Arthur took a drink of the water. "Did you report her missing?"

"What for? She's a teenager. She's stayed away before."

"She's probably scared to death." Arthur said, replacing the cap and rubbing the cold bottle over his forehead. "Does her phone have one of those tracking apps?"

She backed away from the window and stood with her arms crossed, her breasts testing the strength of the remaining two snaps of the tank top. "No." She huffed. "We're lucky we even have those damn phones."

Arthur took another gulp and said, "Is there anywhere she might go? Someone she might turn to for help if she were in trouble?"

"Ah, fuck, I don't know," she said. "I don't get too much involved in her life. Kids today just want to be left alone. So I left her alone."

Arthur said nothing.

"Don't look at me like that." She went back to the window for another quick peek. "You think I didn't watch my kid enough, follow her every damn move. Well fuck you! I don't need your judgment. I get enough of that from the ignorant whites I meet." She checked the wall clock hanging above the doorway into the back bedroom. "You better get the hell outta here before my husband gets home. You've had your water and I've answered your questions."

Arthur gulped down the last of the bottle's water, put the cap back on, and set it on the worn laminated countertop of the kitchenette.

"Do you know where Tiffany Maldonado lives? Maybe her mother might know something."

"She hasn't been home either," Jennifer Peshlakai's mother told him. "I called her the night Jenny didn't come home. You can't separate those two, you know? BFFs and all that shit."

Arthur thought for a moment, then asked again but in a different way. "Do the girls and the Tabaaha boys have any mutual friends at the high school? Somebody they might turn to?"

Arthur watched her check the window again and wondered what it was like to live in that kind of fear. He remembered Sharon doing a story on domestic violence among Native people. Her research showed that Native American women suffered from a domestic abuse rate 85 percent higher than the national average. But those were just statistics; this was right in front of him.

There were no bruises he could see, beyond those on her hand, and those were probably defensive. But that didn't mean they weren't on other parts of her body covered by her clothes. "How long has your husband abused you?"

Jennifer Peshlakai's mother looked startled. "He's never—"

"That's not what the black and blue on your hands say. You could always pack a bag and go to the Family Crisis Center or the Navajo United Methodist Center, both of which are nearby in Farmington."

"I told you, he's never touched me." She looked at her hands briefly. "I took a spill on the ATV the other day. That's all. I don't need CYFD."

Arthur thought hard about his next question. Because if he were right, the Children, Youth, and Families Department was her next step. "Has Jennifer's father ever abused her?"

"Stepfather," she corrected. "And fuck you! Who the fuck you think you are anyway?"

"It's obvious you're afraid of your husband, or you wouldn't be checking the window so often. I'm guessing you keep your bruises well hidden. If he's ever abused Jennifer, then I'm also willing to bet there's someone at school she confides in who may know where she might be hiding." He noticed her begin to pace like a caged animal. "Tell me who you think that person might be, and I'll leave right now."

She grabbed a pack of cigarettes and a lighter from a kitchen drawer and lit one, nervously. Shutting the drawer, she tossed the pack and lighter on the dirty countertop.

"Besides those two Tabaaha boys, there was this one kid she hung around with." Arthur watched her take a drag and hold it in. He held his own breath waiting for her to exhale. When she did, a gray fog filled the close air of the trailer as she spoke. "There was a Filipino kid … Jason Aquino, I think."

"Do you know where he lives?"

"Hell, no," she declared. "Somewhere across the river is all I know. They had a couple of classes together." She took another drag on the cigarette and pointed her chin in the direction of the school. "Why don't you go there and bug them?" Before he could answer, she opened the trailer door and blew the cloud of toxins outside. "Now get the hell out. I told you what you wanted to know."

Arthur nodded, pushed open the storm door, and trotted down the few steps to the ground. He let out his captive breath and took a gulp of fresh air that tasted like slow-moving river water. Just as he hit the ground, he heard the trailer door slam shut behind him. Without looking back, he walked to the Bronco and climbed in. After the engine's eight cylinders fired, he pulled the shifter into reverse and began to back up just as a gray Chevy pickup pulled in behind him and blocked him. A white man of average height and build jumped out, ran to his driver's-side door and yanked it open.

Arthur had just enough time to slap the shifter back into park before he was hauled from the Bronco and slammed against its side. "Why the hell you coming out of my house, asshole? I don't like guys coming outta my house when I'm not there. It makes me think bad thoughts."

Arthur remained calm and went to work quickly. Using the strength of his upper body, both of his arms rose abruptly, taking his attacker off guard. He extricated himself from the man's grip and gave a sharp knee to the groin which doubled him over enough so Arthur could drive his right elbow hard into the left side of the man's face, causing his head to snap sharply to the right. Quickly clasping his two fists together, Arthur brought them down on the base of the man's neck, driving him to the ground.

As Arthur stood while his attacker rolled on the ground, he glanced at the laced window of the trailer. He saw Jenifer Peshlakai's mother watching as the man—or at least who Arthur now presumed was the stepfather—continued to rock in pain. Arthur knelt down and grabbed a fistful of hair and jerked his bruised and bleeding head backward.

"You know what I don't like?" Arthur said. "I don't like assholes who get off on beating up women. So when I find your stepdaughter, if she tells me you've ever touched her, you'll have more to worry about than Child Protective Services. You'll have me coming back here and dragging your worthless ass out of that bed and separating you from your balls with my sheep shears!" Arthur's hand tightened further around the fist-ful of brown hair. "Do you understand?"

The stepfather made meager yet agonizing noises through his pain, muffled a bit by the tears he was shedding and the blood that was coming from his mouth. He still did not reply to Arthur's question. So he asked again, this time using his other hand to put a vice grip on his genitals.

"I said, do you understand? A simple 'yes' will do."

Jenifer Peshlakai's mother watched attentively … smiling.

"Yes!" the man cried out.

Arthur released his grip and let the stepfather fall backward onto the hard ground. "Have a nice day."

Arthur stood and climbed back into the Bronco, quickly pulled the shifter into gear, and drove in a tight circle on the lot before heading back up 6400 wondering if had just made things worse. Probably not, Arthur grinned. Who was the guy going to tell? Besides, the whole trip may have been a dead end anyway. He wondered if perhaps Sharon knew anyone at Kirt-land Central High. He decided to have her see if she could find out where Jason Aquino lived while he made the drive toward Counselor. It was about time he visited his old acquaintance and got some answers.

CHAPTER EIGHT

It only took a couple of hours for Arthur to drive south on High-way 550 to Counselor. The pavement that stretched out before him was a long black ribbon that had been transformed into gray by the unrelenting sun and heat of several summers. And he couldn't help but notice how the New Mexican winters had already brought out the road crews to fill the jagged cracks in its smooth surface with ribbons of black tar that seemed to snake their way south like so many keloid scars. He had rolled down all the windows in the truck in an effort to keep the dry air moving through it, but his efforts still failed to keep him from overheating. He slowed and turned right onto BIA 537 across from the Apache Nugget Casino and headed southwest, past the scarred remnants of the barrow pit, and drove toward Deer Mesa. It was close to six o'clock in the evening, and Arthur could see that the moon had joined the sun in its dance across the sky. Three more hours and night would take over. Maybe things would cool down then.

The Desert Patriots compound sat on a portion of ground higher than the desert landscape that surrounded it, but far less than the 7,509 feet of Deer Mesa, which loomed imposingly in the near distance. As Arthur approached, he made a note of the security cameras strategically placed at intervals on the high chain-link fence and nestled among the shining razor wire that surrounded the forty-acre property. Guards dressed in desert camo and assault rifles walked the perimeter with Doberman Pinschers on taut leashes, their black-and-blue coats shimmering in the sunlight like muscled silk. Arthur drove toward the gate. One guard stood motionless, a red Doberman sitting at alert at his side, waiting for the command to strike. Another guard approached the Bronco confidently but slowly, his Bushwhacker EX-15 angled across his chest at a downward slope with the neck strap.

The burly guard stopped a few feet away from Arthur's open window, right hand wrapped around the grip of his rifle, his index finger positioned at the ready just above the trigger. Arthur noticed the safety was off. "Looks like you're lost, Indian. You lost?" Looking back at the other guard, he remarked, "I think he's lost."

Arthur looked at the stubbled face below the dark sunglasses and desert camo floppy hat and said calmly, "I'm here to see Elias Dayton." While making sure to keep an eye on the other guard through the dusty windshield, Arthur noticed one of the security cameras panning in his direction. The camera stopped to allow the viewer to watch the scene unfold. "I have some questions for him."

The guard huffed and smiled. "What makes you think he wants to talk to you, Indian?" He glanced back at the other guard who was grinning and then back at Arthur. "Fucking wagon burner."

Arthur inhaled deeply and let it out slowly before saying, "I bet you played Cowboys and Indians when you were a kid. And I bet you were always the cowboy." He watched as the smile disappeared from the guard's face. "Well, I played that game too. And you know what? I always ended up kicking the cowboy's ass."

The guard pursed his lips at the same time his left hand gripped the EX's handguard, but he stopped short of moving his finger through the trigger guard. Arthur watched the stubbled guard's head tilt as someone spoke to him through the earpiece that pigtailed out of his left ear. He saw a hand move to the push-to-talk button on his fatigues. "Yes, sir," the guard said. "Of course, sir," the guard said. The guard then turned to the second man stationed by the fence. "Let him through!"

The second guard reached inside the guard hut and the chain-link gate slowly slid open.

"Go straight ahead until to you come to a V," the burly guard instructed. "Take the left fork. You'll see a tan cinderblock building on your right. That's where you'll be met." He smirked. "Have a good day … Indian."

Arthur had grown up knowing people with hatred in their hearts. Some were Bilagáana and some were Native, and some were members of other types of people who inhabited the planet, but all held within them a prejudice that had festered throughout their lives. Anger and hatred run deep, he reasoned, even today with those too young to understand where it comes from or why it is proliferated by shallow minds. The anger seems to vary by age and education, but one can choose to either let the anger build up within them until it becomes all that they are, absorbing their soul so that all they can see is the hatred committed against them or their race by others, or one can choose to let it exist in history and not become the reason for their own present discontent.

As he drove slowly through the gate and into the compound, he could feel every eye watching him. Never mind them, he told himself, his people and the other nations of the land now called the United States were older than America itself. They had always had people looking at them. Never mind that the Europeans had claimed all the land as their own through a series of violent eradications and broken treaties. Never mind that the great push westward for the settlers was nothing more than their way to create a so-called civilized world—a colonized world. A false world.

When Arthur pulled up and parked at the tan building, he was met by two more guards dressed the same as the two at the gate, the same as everyone else he had seen in the compound. Turning off the engine, he climbed out and shut the door and was greeted immediately by a guard who spun him around and began patting him down. The other guard stood watch, assault rifle at the ready. Arthur could see the sweat running down their faces and the staining in their armpits and on their chests and backs. He smirked to himself, remembering the ungodly heat of the Registan Desert of Afghanistan. The Bilagáana couldn't stand it there either.

The pat down completed, the two men guided him into the building and down a long, empty corridor, one in front and one behind. It had been years since Arthur had sat across from Elias Dayton, and he wondered if he was still the cocky little prick he remembered him to be. Short on brains and long on arrogance. When the men stopped at a gray metal door, the guard who had done the patting down knocked three times hard with a fist.

"Enter!" the recognizable voice barked.

Tweedledee opened the door while Tweedledum pushed him inside then looked to the man behind the desk for further instructions.

The man was Elias Dayton himself, and he simply motioned in the guards' direction with his chin. "Leave us."

Arthur heard the door close behind him. The figure sitting behind the large desk had put on some weight in the years since they had last met, and his face had now taken on a more mature look. His hair appeared to be a little thinner but not much, Arthur figuring it was probably the haircut. The formerly longish, unkempt hair of Elias Dayton had now become the finely coiffed look of a businessman. But there was something else Arthur noticed: this time Elias Dayton's eyes held a more knowledgeable and measured gaze.

"Come and sit down, Mr. Nakai," Dayton said, waving a hand toward two tufted leather chairs in front of his desk. "Would you like something to drink? A whiskey perhaps?"

Arthur walked toward the chairs positioned in front of the massive desk at forty-five-degree angles. The room itself was decorated a little too much on the dark side for his taste, but it had all the trappings of acquired power. An American flag stood draped on a pole to the left of the desk and a Desert Patriots flag with an eagle clutching two snakes dangled from a pole to the right. Arthur refused the offer of a drink with a shake of his head and sat.

Dayton tossed his pen onto some papers in front of him and looked at the man sitting before him. "It's been, what, eight, ten years since you sent us packing at the border?"

"Ten," Arthur said.

Dayton nodded, clasped his hands in front of him, elbows on the desktop. "You and your lot didn't want any *real* help did you? You didn't want to *handle* the problem, you just wanted to pacify it."

Arthur balanced the side of his right boot on his left knee and used his left hand to keep it from moving. "You were welcomed down there along with the rest of the civilian observers as long as you played by the rules that were set down." Arthur cocked his head. "You didn't. What part of observe and report did you have trouble with?"

Elias Dayton chuckled. "You guys were simply a Band-Aid on a gushing wound. A wound that keeps pumping illegals into this country like holes in a garden soaker. Hell, man, Mexicans are renting their own children for border crossings for as much as eighty bucks a head! We've got CBP agents scouring train yards looking at the bellies of trains for UDAs hiding underneath them. And we've got over a hundred thousand pounds of marijuana and thousands of illegals moving through fucking drain pipes every year, or did you forget about that?"

Arthur picked up on the soft ticking of a mantel clock somewhere in the room off to his left. He heard the click and then the whirring of its mechanism as its small hammers began striking the chimes in Westminster fashion.

"I didn't come here to discuss immigration problems with you," Arthur said. "I came here to ask you if you or your men had anything to do with two boys who were shot and killed out by Flat Iron Rock yesterday."

No reaction. The clock's chimes faded.

"I heard about that," Dayton said finally. "Very unfortunate. I was saddened to read about it in this morning's paper. But why should you think we would have had anything to do with that?"

"Because of the way they were killed," Arthur told him. "It took skill. It took someone with a steady hand and a sniper rifle. Something I'm sure most of your people here have had a lot of range-time practice with."

"I see." Dayton sat back and drummed his fingertips on the desktop. "And *why* would I have done this? I see no advantage in killing two Indian boys."

"You tell me," Arthur said. "Maybe you want to keep the fire burning in the bellies of the people who see us as less than human, as pests that still need to be exterminated. Maybe you want to push your agenda to gain more recruits. Or maybe there's a connection between you providing security to NMX for its wells and drilling rigs and their need to acquire more land."

Dayton scoffed audibly, stopped drumming his fingers. "There have always been people in this country hating other people for no other reason than that they have been told that those people are the root of all their problems. And people are always joining my company, but not because of hate. And, yes, we do provide security for NMX because of all the Water Keepers running around protesting and keeping their workers— honest men and women with families—from making a living." He paused, a disgusted look on his face. "Do you know how much time and money would be lost if we allowed those Water Keepers to fuck things up by protesting here for almost a year like they did in Standing Rock over the DAPL?" He smirked. "'Defend the Sacred,' my ass. All they did was cause trouble and delay the inevitable and leave a fucking mess behind."

"But they were right," Arthur said. "Water *is* life. The Dakota Access Pipelines were, and are, threatening the water table up there just like they are here and everywhere else they get buried. Already there have been some underground gas lines across the country that have ruptured. All you have to do is google it to find out. What people like you don't understand is that what little water we have out here is precious to us. Your friends come in here with empty promises of prosperity for those who lease their land so that they can shove a hundred more needles in the ground over the next five years and continue to poison the aquifer with their chemical fracking. People like you will never understand."

"Understand what?"

"That once you carry your own water, you learn the value of every drop."

"Don't tell me you're one of those water assholes now?" Dayton shook his head. "It's not my job to worry about any of that shit. What *is* my job is protecting those workers and those drilling rigs and those wells."

"I get it," Arthur said. "And when all is said and done, and the land is poisoned and we're left with nothing but worthless ground, they'll simply take their profits and leave us with soil that is no good to anyone because they had no intension of cleaning up their mess correctly in the first place."

"Well, it's your fucking people that have been snapping at the chance to earn some cash," Dayton countered. "Now they finally have some money in their pockets and can improve their third-world lives."

"Not all of them," Arthur stressed. "Only the ones who went through the allotment process managed by the federal government and own their land can lease it. The rest of the land is owned by the BLM and other groups. And the rest of my people that don't get lease payments just get to sit back and watch the dust rise into the air and hear the groan of big rigs hauling away the benefits of raping our land." Arthur crossed his arms. "There are over twenty-four hundred oil and gas wells sucking all they can get from underground from Bloomfield down to Cuba, while the rest of the country doesn't even understand what the hell is going on out here."

"The rest of the country," Dayton said arrogantly, "doesn't really *care* what the hell's going on out here. They only care about what the media tells them to care about. And right now, that happens to be something entirely different. What I care about is keeping your people away from those wells and drilling platforms in the corridor so that my employer's people can do what they're being paid to do."

"I didn't realize beating the hell out of Natives was part of their job description."

Dayton smirked. "I'll admit there have been some ...

altercations involving some of the workers from the man-camps, but that's because your people have been causing trouble for the workers by protesting the worksites, blocking roadways, that kind of shit."

Arthur decided to push a button and see what type of reaction he would get. "I heard one attack took place at gas station, far from a rig or any camp. I heard a man was beaten severely. I also heard that no one has seen him since."

Dayton shrugged. "Well, I haven't heard of any such incident." Then he grinned and added, "And they probably haven't been seen because they went out and tied one on and are still fucking drunk, or they're off somewhere with some broad they shacked up with. They'll show up when whoever it is kicks them out of the hogan."

Arthur felt the muscles of his jaw bunch, but before he could respond, Dayton's cell phone rang on his desk. "Excuse me," he said as he fisted it with his right hand and held it to his ear. "What?"

A muffled voice on the other end muttered something Arthur couldn't understand. Dayton's face remained a blanket of controlled indifference. "Well, make sure it's mounted securely and ready to go. We don't need these people making any more trouble and hurting production." He ended the call, tossed the phone onto the desk, and looked at Arthur. "I think we're done here, Nakai." He stood. "I can assure you that none of my people beat anyone up or killed anyone, and NMX knows everything that's going on with its workers and its installations. Now, if you'll excuse me …"

Arthur stood. "I'll find my own way out."

Dayton's eyes followed him as he walked across the quiet carpeting of the office. Once the office door closed behind Arthur, Dayton reached for his cell phone again and tapped a contact as he worked through the maze of possibilities now running through his calculating mind. He continued to stare at the closed office door as the call rang through.

The voice that spilled into Dayton's ear was calm and precisely metered. "Yes?"

"I have a special job for you," Dayton said. "We have a problem."

CHAPTER NINE

"So what time do you expect to be home?" Sharon asked. The Bronco was bouncing and swaying its way down the graded dirt road from the Desert Patriots compound toward Highway 550. "Probably late," Arthur said. "Did your contact at the school give you Jason Aquino's address?"

"Yes, I have it. What's it worth to ya?" Sharon was talking over the usual newsroom clamor around her that Arthur had come to expect over the years. It never seemed to decrease, only intensify as the world became a more divided and political and ever so complicated place to live.

"Just be naked when I get there," Arthur replied.

"Ooh, I like it when you're assertive."

"You just like it when I'm firm."

"Anything less is disappointing, baby." Sharon chuckled then added, "He lives in Nenahnezad. I'll text you the directions."

"Nenahnezad? That's two hours back the way I came. Wish I'd known that before I left Kirtland."

"Hey, my source only just called me back," she informed

him, then added jokingly, "Stop complaining. You're lucky I still put up with you and love you so much."

"Just give me the address," Arthur replied. "I'll use the GPS on my phone to find it."

"You do know," Sharon said, "most *new* vehicles come with GPS navigation built in? And only you could grow attached to that rust bucket."

"Hey, this Bronco's a classic," Arthur joked. "And those rust spots give it character."

Sharon laughed. "Only in your mind."

"At least I don't drive a pregnant banana."

"At least I have GPS," Sharon reminded him. "Nenahnezad is a CDP community, babe. Your phone GPS may have trouble helping you navigate a Census Designated Place. Just follow the directions I'm sending you, okay?"

"Okay. But if I get a chance to talk to this kid," Arthur told her, "I won't be home till about nine or nine thirty."

Sharon sighed. "Well, it won't be the first time I ate dinner alone."

Arthur grinned. "Now who's complaining?"

He could sense the smirk on her face when she said, "Oh, shut up."

Arthur felt the two front-end stabilizers keeping the big tires of the Bronco in check as his hands gripped the wheel a little bit tighter in an effort to maintain control. "I know those girls are scared and hiding somewhere," he said. "No one has seen them since that night, and if this kid knows anything about them, hopefully he can lead us to them so we can find out what they know."

"*We?*" Sharon said.

"Me and Jake. If I find out, I want the Navajo Nation Police to pick them up. They can question them and keep them safe.

I have a feeling there's more at stake here than just the lives of two innocent boys."

"How so?" Sharon said.

"After talking with Elias Dayton, the feeling I had in my gut has gone from bad to worse."

"I just wish you didn't have to check this kid out right now," Sharon said. "The sooner you get here, the faster you're going to be allowed into the big top."

Arthur smiled. "Okay, can we stop with the circus references now? I think we've worn them out." He spoke softly when he said, "*Ayóó 'áníinish 'ní.*"

Sharon's voice turned quiet at the words *I love you.* He knew she adored hearing them, even reveled in their simplistic beauty, because they meant so much more now than ever before.

He waited.

"*Ayóó 'áníinish 'ní, she 'ashkii,*" she replied. "See you when you get home."

"I'm looking forward to it," Arthur said.

* * *

Arthur shot the Bronco across Highway 550 and parked under the large portico by the gas pumps of the Apache Nugget Casino's Travel Center. It didn't take him long to gas up, grab a snack of beef sticks and a cold bottle of sweet tea before getting on his way again. By the time he rolled into Nenahnezad on BIA Route 36, it was twenty minutes past eight and the sun was sinking toward nightfall with all the fire and splendor the Creator could paint with his masterful brush.

After turning off Route 36 and burping across the cattle guard, he rolled down to the three-way stop, past the pink modular home Sharon's directions told him about. He turned right toward Fruitland, the direction confirmed by the green state road sign, and soon felt the pavement begin to slope as he drove past a motley crew of derelict trucks and cars scattered haphazardly among the sage and scrub, past the scattered ramshackle homes to where he eventually found himself rolling under a string of power lines before driving through an excavated section of earth as the road curved down toward the next left turn on Sharon's directions.

He paused briefly by the concrete drainage ditch to watch the murky brown water move off to parts unknown. After pulling on the headlight knob, he turned left and drove through the Chapter community of less than eight hundred.

Seeing communities like this always took him back to his days growing up on the rez. He remembered a life of taking baths at the watering hole while his father pumped the freezing water as he stood under it, bathing as quickly as he could because they, like everyone else, had no running water. He remembered pumping the water for his father, just as he remembered living with no electricity until he had joined the Marines and gotten out of the grip of rez life. Looking around, it seemed like nothing had changed in the last twenty-seven years, even with all the good intentions of others and government dollars. And that truly saddened him enough to wonder if there would ever be a time when things would change for the better.

The farther he traveled the more he found himself moving into Jason Aquino's world. The small farms were behind him now, but the poverty ahead of him was gut-wrenching. Since the road system that ran through Nenahnezad was a mixture of tribal roads, county roads, and Bureau of Indian Affairs roads, it was hard to know where one ended and another began. But he followed Sharon's directions to the letter, ending up on BIA 365. To the north was the San Juan River, to the south was the long-stretching Navajo Coal Mine, operated by the Navajo Coal Company, and somewhere between the two lay Jason Aquino's single-wide manufactured home.

It wasn't long before he turned off 365 and drove through the wire fencing that surrounded the Aquino property. His headlights managed to illuminate a string of clothes flapping in the eighty-three-degree breeze. Arthur wagered the clothes had already been dried by the earlier heat of the day and were now simply enjoying the mild evening. Another house of equal proportions sat behind Aquino's, but he saw no lights on inside and no vehicle parked outside of it. Arthur parked the Bronco by a 1970s white Nova. It was blotchy with gray and brown primer and sitting at the end of the Aquino home. He killed the lights and engine and let the hollow sound of the door echo as it slammed shut behind him.

At the front door he paused, thinking that an unexpected knock at this time of night was not something that would be welcome. He eyed the primered Nova again, took a deep breath, and risked the knock. A minute later the door opened and someone he could only assume to be Jason Aquino's father stood looking down at him. Arthur noted the brown skin, the straight black hair, the flatness of the straight nose, and the dark-brown eyes that stared questioningly down from under narrowish brows.

"Yes?" the man said in a Filipino accent, "What do you want?"

"My name is Arthur Nakai, and I'd like to speak with your son, Jason. Is he home?"

The man's eyes scanned the dirt yard, the flapping laundry, and the occasional traffic that passed by on BIA 365, before settling back on Arthur. "What's this about? You police?"

"No, I'm not the police. Just a concerned friend of a family who experienced a tragedy." Arthur kept his hands at his sides and made no quick movements. "I'm investigating the murder of the two boys out by Flat Iron Rock. Maybe you've heard about it?"

"Yes, I have," the man said. "A terrible thing. But what does that have to do with my son?"

"I was told that your son is friends with two girls the boys hung out with. Jennifer Peshlakai and Tiffany Maldonado." Arthur remained calm and polite. "I need to see if he knows where the girls might be. They haven't been seen since the boys were killed, and their parents are worried. You would be worried too if Jason were missing."

The man called out something in Filipino over his shoulder, and a young man of around seventeen appeared behind him. The man spoke more words in his native language, and Jason Aquino nodded. "This is Mr. Nakai. You need to answer his questions. Tell him what you know," his father prodded, grabbing him by his arm and moving him to the forefront of the conversation in the doorway.

"Hello, Jason," Arthur said, holding out a hand. Jason shook it and returned the greeting. "I'm looking for two girls I think you know, Tiffany Maldonado and Jennifer Peshlakai. Do you have any idea where they are? Their parents are worried."

Jason stood still, his arms tight at his sides and his hands stuffed into the front pockets of his jeans. Nervous. His father shoved a hand into the back of his left shoulder, causing him to lose his footing for a second before reclaiming it.

"If you know, tell him!" he commanded.

"I—I do know where they are," Jason said sheepishly, staring at his feet. "They're scared and made me promise not to tell anyone."

"That's good, Jason," Arthur told him calmly. "You're a good friend. But the girls need my help. I need to find them. Did the girls tell you anything about what happened that night?"

He shook his head, still not wanting to hold eye contact, as if that would make breaking his promise to his friends even more untrustworthy. "They didn't want to in case the person who did it found them. The less I knew, the safer I'd be, they said." Arthur nodded his head approvingly. "I see." He paused. The boy looked away. "Jason?" Arthur coaxed. "Where are they?"

The boy looked at Arthur momentarily, but did not respond. "Jason," Arthur prodded delicately. "Where can I find them?"

Again, his father's hand shoved his son in the back.

Jason said, "You know where Cathedral Cliff is?"

Arthur nodded. "It's that large volcanic formation out by Table Mesa off 491. Kind of like Shiprock, but shorter."

"Yes. That's it. There is a small cave at the back of Cathedral Cliff. Me and a few of my friends went exploring out there one day, and we found it." Jason gave Arthur a fleeting glance. "We thought we might find a skeleton or something cool in there, but there was nothing. Just a cave. So when they came to me for help, I knew I could put them there so they would be safe. I've made sure they have food and blankets and those things you break that warm your hands and feet. I even gave them some flashlights." His father's hand was on his son's shoulder now, encouraging him. Arthur could see a look of pride on his face. "They're scared, Mr. Nakai. *Very* scared. They're afraid the killer will come for them." He shrugged. "But I told them, if the killer had no idea where to look, why did they think he would find them?"

Ah, the logic of the young.

"When did you bring them those supplies?"

"The night it happened," Jason said. "They called me all frantic, and I snuck out and met them at the Wendy's in Kirtland. If you have the police check, they'll find Tiffany Maldonado's Bronco II parked over in the Encore Motel lot. I was planning to go out to Cathedral Cliff every couple of days to check on them."

Arthur reached out a hand, and the boy shook it again. "Thank you, Jason. You did the right thing. The girls are going to be all right, and it's all because of you."

Jason Aquino smiled bashfully, and his father grinned with affirmation that his son had handled himself honorably, even if it took a little prodding. Arthur pulled his cell phone from his shirt pocket as he walked back to his truck. When the screen lit up, his thumb found Jake Bilagody's number. Arthur knew he would still be behind his desk at this hour since he was still sharing his duties while acting as Window Rock chief until they could locate a replacement. Jake had never been one to shirk his duty in twenty-seven years, and he probably never would. Not even on his last day—whenever that would be.

Jake answered, "Bilagody."

"Tell me where you are on the Tabaaha boys' murders."

* * *

Jake rocked back in his office chair and used his feet to oscillate from side to side. "I've got a man checking on what stores sell those boots you mentioned back at the site—what did you call it? A hide? Anyway, he hasn't come back with anything useful yet. And we never recovered any shell casings, so we still have to go with Mendoza's guesstimate on that. We've got a list of around forty or so folks who own the type of rifle used that we're trying to work through from Shiprock to Farmington to Navajo City." Jake's pause was drawn out. "Why don't you tell me why you're calling."

"I'm going to give you some information because there's too much at stake not to." Arthur got into the Bronco and fired it up. "Did you know there were two girls with the Tabaaha boys that night?"

Jake rocked his chair forward and rested his elbows on his desk. "I did not. How do you know?"

"Because I went back out to the crime scene this morning and did some more sign cutting. I found two separate sets of footprints among all the ones NNP left behind—both the size for teenage girls."

"No shit?"

"Then I spoke with Margaret—"

"We tried that this afternoon," Jake interrupted, disregarding the Navajo rule of never disrespecting anyone by interrupting them, "but she was so far in the bag we couldn't get anything coherent out of her. That was so sad to see."

"Well, I was there before you and got the names of two girls who were with the boys that night." Arthur rattled off the names and where to locate the Bronco II. He could hear Jake scribbling fast. "Are you ready for the best part?"

"I'm listening."

"Do you have anyone out patrolling tonight around Cathedral Cliff?"

"I'd have to check with dispatch. Why?"

"Because I just spoke to a boy who's been hiding the girls out there to keep them safe."

"What the hell! Why didn't they come to the police?"

"Because they're just kids, Jake. Scared teenage kids." Arthur turned on his headlights and shifted into reverse, backed up a quarter turn, put it back into drive and flung dirt before chirping the tires back onto the asphalt of BIA 365. "I suggest you get a car out there right now. I'm going home to go to bed." He wasn't about to tell Jake why. "If they give you anything useful, let me know in the morning."

"Wait, so who told you where they are?"

"A friend of theirs. That's all you need to know." Arthur's

eyelids began to fall over his eyes like heavy curtains. He forced himself to stay awake and alert. "I'll talk to you tomorrow. I've got about forty-five minutes to get home and really intend to make them count."

"All right," Jake said. "I'll get with you tomorrow."

The moment the call ended, Arthur stuffed the phone into the cup holder in the center console, next to the half-drank bottle of sweet tea, and stuck his head out of the truck window. The cooler night air felt good and crisp against his face, the wind chilling his skin with its smoothed edges as he moved through the night. If he smoked, this would be where he would tap out a cigarette, punch the lighter, wait for it to pop, and hold the glowing round ball to the tip and breathe in all those wonderful carcinogens that would keep him awake. But he didn't smoke anymore. That habit had gone away like his love for books. He had started reading and stopped smoking during his down time in the Marines. He really needed to pick up the reading part again. After all, he had received his first novel, a Robert B. Parker mystery, from another soldier who got it in a care package from home. Back then he had needed something that would take him to another world—Boston, in this case—and put him firmly in the gumshoes that roamed a different combat zone than he found himself in. After he was stateside, he kept it up for a few years, collecting classics and every novel he could find concerning the famous Massachusetts detective. All he had now, however, was a half-empty bottle of sugared tea and the night air. *Guess that'll have to do.*

Arthur pulled his head back in, downed the remaining tea, screwed on the cap, and stuck it back in the second cup holder. Then he picked up the phone and called the number of the one person he knew would be waiting up for him.

"I think you should know," Sharon said, "I'm lying here

naked watching some ridiculous movie just so I won't fall asleep before you get here."

Arthur smiled. "A movie?"

"Can't think of anything better to do," Sharon said, then added in a playfully sarcastic tone, "No, wait. I can, but you're not here."

"I should be home in twenty-five," Arthur said. "Hold that thought."

The splintering of fiberglass that blew across the interior of the Bronco pelted the back of Arthur's head and neck and stung like a swarm of mosquitoes all drilling his skin at once. His reaction was instinctive, a flinch and hunch of the shoulders and a ducking of the head, all while managing to keep a firm grip on the steering wheel. The instant the shot had ripped through the Bronco's hardtop, he had dropped the phone to the floorboard. From that moment on it became a surreal mixture of Sharon's voice screaming through the phone's tiny speaker and a heightened sensory level consuming him, one that he hadn't felt since his days on patrol in the Middle East.

He hadn't been shot at in a vehicle since the combat zone, and he knew what it sounded like because it was impossible to forget. Instantly he heard the driver's-side front tire blow with a pop and felt the steering wheel jerk sharply to the left. Sharon's voice—frightened and disembodied—continued to scream at his feet as the engine roared and the truck rocked with the sudden loss of stability. He overcorrected the wheel and found himself heading for the rough edge of the road where the pavement dropped off a good three or four inches on the right. In a frantic rush to avoid rocketing down the embankment to whatever fate awaited him, he gave a quick tug to the steering wheel, shooting the truck back over the inside lane and bounding over the small curb of the concrete median that separated the east- and westbound lanes. The shredding Mudder tire had begun ripping at the truck's fender well as it flopped around, making thumping sounds as it fiercely tore away at the metal. Arthur's eyes squinted as the truck took him across oncoming traffic, sending the approaching cars and trucks braking and scattering as if they were avoiding a lunatic kid on a bumper car ride.

Arthur's biceps were pumping from adrenaline and worked the wheel deliberately as the disintegrating tire separated from the truck and wobbled through the air awkwardly, disappearing into the darkness. Sparks flew as the spinning rim met the pavement as he struggled to maintain his quickly fading control, the Bronco's headlights now bringing into view the advancing mound of wedge-shaped earth he was approaching.

The truck rumbled up the mound and rotated to its left before taking flight. Arthur pulled his hands from the wheel and crossed them over his chest as the truck spun in the air. When the back of the Bronco's roof impacted the ground, the rear window shattered, forcing the truck's velocity to quickly slam the roof and front end into the earth. Arthur's back wrenched as the grill guard dug into the hard-packed terrain and compressed the truck's front end, bending the hood into a crushed accordion. Arthur felt the back of his head slam against the headrest before the resulting g-force pushed his chin into his sternum and his legs cracked against the underside of the dash, his feet contorting against the pedals as he watched the windshield spiderweb and felt the sting of glass fragments pelting his face as he covered his eyes with his hands.

It was all happening in slow motion.

And then everything stopped.

The truck rocked back onto its roof and laid there still, one headlight shining off into the dust-filled, shadowy night. All

Arthur could think of now that the truck rested on its back was *thank god for the roll bar.*

The Ford engine that had raged as the truck launched off the ridge now droned on at idle speed. He reached for the key and switched off the engine, his weakening arm falling back to him. He looked around through blurry eyes, blood now spotting his face and hands where the glass had cut into them and running from his chin into his mouth and nostrils. He forced red air from his nose and red spit from his mouth just as he felt his mind growing dim, his body growing weak, and his vision slowly fading … and then everything turned to a nice, comfortable shade of black.

CHAPTER TEN

Darkness surrounded Arthur Nakai as he felt a strange wind begin to blow across the shadowy world he found himself wandering through. He knew immediately it was *Niłch'i Diyin*, the Holy Wind of the Dark World that he was taught about as a child. Soon he found himself standing, still and quiet, watching in sheer amazement as the Mist People, who had no certain form of their own, but could assume the shape of bird or beast or reptile, began to move over the Dark World. *This is the time before the earth even existed*, he told himself. *Before the concept of man and woman had even transformed themselves into their present forms, away from simple male and female beings. It must be.* He had heard the Creation story told to him by his paternal grandfather many times while growing up. But *why* was he here? Why should he be allowed to witness such a sacred event? Why would the Creator show him the vision of the beginning of his own people?

He bowed his head, feeling unworthy of this vision that was being bestowed upon him. When he lifted his head, he noticed he was now standing on a small island that floated in the center of four seas. The Mist People could not see him and were busy going about their work. He watched quietly as First Man and First Woman were formed. He saw First Man build a fire using only a crystal, while First Woman did the same using only a piece of turquoise. Arthur's vision was like that of an eagle. He could see that both First Man and First Woman observed each other's fires from a distance. He watched as First Man searched three times in the darkness for her turquoise flame but could not locate it. On his fourth journey, however, Arthur observed First Man tear a branch off the only pine tree he could see for miles and hold it up to indicate where the other light blazed. Arthur followed First Man through the darkness to a home where grayish smoke rose into the air. He fell to his knees as First Woman and First Man met for the first time, drawn to each other by their fire, just as he had been drawn to Sharon.

Soon afterward, several other beings arrived to populate the First World, including the Great-Coyote-Who-Was-Formed-in-the-Water, called First Angry, and the Wasp People along with a multitude of other creatures. They were followed by the beings known as spider ants and black ants. Soon came many other creatures to inhabit the land of the First World including Spider Man and Spider Woman and Salt Man and Salt Woman. As Arthur kept quiet and watched intently, he soon noticed that this world was beginning to be too small to maintain such a large number of creatures, and he watched in amazement as they began fighting amongst themselves. They fought so much that the creatures ended up crawling out of the darkness through a passageway that had been revealed to them in the east.

Arthur quickly followed.

When they emerged into the Second World, the Blue World, Arthur found himself mesmerized by the many creatures that appeared before him, the various blue-gray furry mammals and the many feathered beings, including the blue swallows. It did not take long, however, for the beings from the First World to offend *Táshchózhii*, the Swallow Chief, and there was more fighting and killing. So much so that the Swallow Chief banished them from the Blue World. Arthur watched as First Man created a wand using jet and other minerals so that the banished people could walk upon it to the next world using an opening created in the World of Blue Haze in the south.

Again, Arthur eagerly followed.

The bluebird was first to arrive in *Ni' Ḥaltsooí*, the Third or Yellow World. In this world Arthur could see the two rivers that formed a cross upon the land and the Underwater People who lived along them. He saw the six sacred mountains and the Cave Dwellers, but noticed there was no sun in this world either, yet he was still able to see.

Arthur observed that more animal people lived here than in the first two worlds, and he could see the *Kisa'ni*, the ancient people of the pueblo. This time it was not disharmony that drove the people from this new world but rather a tremendous flood unleashed by *Tééhoołtsódi*, the Water Buffalo, after it was learned that Coyote had slipped across where the two rivers met and stolen her two children on behalf of First Woman.

You can never trust Coyote, Arthur remembered his grandfather saying as he recited the story. *He is only out for himself and is the biggest trickster of all.*

As the water swarmed in from all directions, swirling as it rose steadily and quickly, Arthur fled the great flood with the others and emerged into the Fourth World, the White World. As he looked out upon this new world, he saw that it also was covered in water and there were monsters inhabiting it. Still he was surprised that he could not be seen by anyone, not even the monsters. But there he was, as solid a man as he could be, watching life unfold before his very eyes. He saw himself as an imperceptible traveler who had been given the blessed gift of observing everything from the beginning of time.

He watched as the Sacred Mountains were molded into new majestic forms using soil from the original mountains in the Second World. He watched as First Man, First Woman, and the Holy People created the sun that shone brightly in the sky and gave life to all things. He watched them create the moon, the seasons, and the stars that filled the night sky. And he watched in awe as Water Buffalo appeared, her curly wet hair and black horns shining as the water ran from her head. She had come for her two children, the ones stolen from her by Coyote.

It was First Man who stood and asked her why she had followed them into the Fourth World since it was she who had started the great flood. He got no response. Coyote stepped forward and opened his coat to reveal the two stolen children. Water Buffalo snorted. Her eyes blazed. Coyote was given a basket laden with sacred pollens and a crystal. Everyone, including Arthur, watched as Coyote placed the basket between the horns of the great Water Buffalo, and as he did so he informed her that they would give back only the male child, who would be known as the Black Cloud or Male Rain. He would bring with him thunder and lightning. He also instructed Water Buffalo that they would keep the female child, and she would be known as the blue, yellow, and white clouds that would bring the gentle, soothing rains that would moisten the earth and make things grow so that they all might live.

It was here, as Arthur watched and listened, that First Man spoke of this new world being a small and barren land, a land which had been soaked and made useless by the flood of the lower worlds. Arthur hid and watched as First Man planted a large female reed that grew up to the roof of the Fourth World. First Man then tasked two beings to climb the reed and venture into the Fifth World. When they returned, they told great stories of powerful medicines and of a world that was dry. And so, First Man and First Woman then led the people into the Fifth World.

It was at this time Arthur began to feel something soft and familiar surrounding his right hand. He looked down but did not see anything that would make him feel such a sensation. Yet he felt it take hold of him and draw him farther away from the spectacle before him.

Soon a calming mist began to envelop him, and he could see nothing of his surroundings but began to feel every tingle and distinguish every sound. Along with this newfound awareness came a feeling coursing through his body—like tiny fires that had been unleashed to give him just enough pain to feel alive. Throughout this new awakening in the Fifth World, words were being spoken that were stirred into the soup of his brain, more stock to be added to the broth of his subconscious.

He was becoming more aware now the of strange sounds that were filtering into this consciousness, sounds that quickly became more annoying in their monotony, while others seemed comforting in their familiarity. He began to comprehend the warmth that seemed to surround his hand, and his olfactory senses were filled with the delicate aroma of a familiar fragrance. It was *her* fragrance. Sharon's fragrance. And he recognized it instantly.

As he stepped from the mist, his eyes focused on the sterile white room and the perforated ceiling tiles that held the aluminum track of the curtain that had been pulled back against the wall to allow the nurse to perform her duties. She was changing the IV and smiled softly down at him, her blue eyes compassionate in the harshness of the overhead lighting. When he moved his eyes from the nurse, he saw Sharon sitting beside him, tears quietly streaming down her face, her hands clasped like a clamshell around his right hand. He smiled. She smiled, then rested a gentle hand against his wounded and bruised face. She stood carefully and leaned over him, pressed her sweet lips against his with a restrained passion that brought with it a sense of the promise that kept the tiny fires of pain in check. Her tears fell wet against his face, and all he could do was realize the purpose of his vision. It had all been placed there as the path to lead him back to her.

As if the repetitive tones of the EKG monitoring his heart weren't steady and irritating enough, the bulky alligator clip clamped to his index finger added to his annoyance, and the electrodes stuck to his chest made him feel like a guinea pig in a science fiction movie. Sharon sniffled as her face drew away from his, and he saw her look across the room. Arthur turned his head as far as his aching neck would allow and saw Jake Bilagody and John Sykes standing to his left, looking like they were in a museum staring at an abstract painting they couldn't quite figure out. They were also blocking his view of the clear blue sky. The concave design of the hospital seemed to capture the sun as it tried to penetrate his room through the multipaned window behind them.

Jake was the first to step up, his uniform crisp and sharp-edged as always, his gun belt polished and glistening of Kiwi black. In comparison, Arthur noted, Sykes looked like Lee Marvin's stunt double from *The Dirty Dozen*. Arthur also noticed that the reassuring look on Jake's face was trying to mask the hint of reservation that still lingered behind his middle-aged eyes.

"Glad you made it back to the land of the living," Jake said.

Arthur half grinned, still groggy. "How did I get here?" He rolled his head over on the pillow and looked at Sharon again. She had pulled her long black hair into a ponytail that trailed down the back of her orange blouse with the white buttons. "The last thing I remember is being on the phone with you."

"I didn't know what was happening," Sharon confided. "I heard the crash and then nothing. I called Jake the second I lost the call." Sharon's body quaked visibly. "I never want to hear that sound again." She kissed the back of his bruised, alligator-clipped hand softy. "I thought I'd lost you."

Arthur squeezed her hand with the thumb and three free fingers of his right hand, leaving the alligator-clipped index finger extended. "Does Ak'is miss me?"

Sharon smiled. "Of course he does. He was following me all around the house last night before I left to come here. He's probably still sitting on the back porch waiting for you."

Arthur smiled and rolled his head back over to Jake. "How's my truck?"

"The whole front end, radiator, and some other pertinent parts, along with some of the undercarriage, are toast," he said. "The hardtop is beyond repair due to the bullet hole and you landing on it. Hosteen says the frame's bent, and you broke a motor mount so there's a lot of costly work coming your way. And the windshield will need to be replaced. He'll have to order you a new hardtop and can get working on it as soon as we give it to him. Other than that, it's in perfect shape." Jake held up a hand, thwarting Arthur's next question. "We're holding it as evidence because we need to go over it thoroughly before any work gets done."

"Evidence?" Arthur said. "Bullet holes?"

Jake's eyes looked at Sharon, then gave a sideways look to Sykes before landing back on Arthur. "You didn't just blow a tire, my friend. Someone shot at you. And not just to scare you off."

Arthur could feel Sharon's body bristling from the tendons in her hands clamping around his. "Looks like I got close to something, and someone doesn't like it."

"A little too close," Jake agreed. "Forensics pulled the same kind of slug from your truck that we found at the Flat Iron.

Whoever killed Tsela and Tahoma Tabaaha wanted to take you out too."

The nurse finished her task with the IV and quietly left the room, closing the door behind her.

"Hard to believe they missed," Arthur said, then looked at Sykes. "What are you doing here?"

"I have a scanner in my truck. I was visiting someone here in Farmington last night when I heard the call. I figured they'd be bringing you to San Juan Regional." He walked to the foot of the bed and leaned against the wall, crossing his arms. "Didn't wanna be in the way last night, so I texted the guys and told them what happened after I got a room at the Travel Inn."

"You stayed around town just to check on me?"

Sykes shrugged. "Forty bucks for a clean bed and a microwave. Besides, the guys are all worried and brothers always have each other's six."

Arthur fought the throbbing pain in his face and body and grimaced as it tried to take hold of him through the pain meds dripping from the bag above. He noticed Jake working on a thought while he stood there listening to the two men talk. It didn't take him long to verbalize it.

"You two wouldn't mind if I spoke with Arthur alone, would you?"

"Not at all," Sykes said, lifting himself from the wall.

"Of course not," Sharon agreed, letting go of her husband's bruised hand. "John," she offered, "you want to grab a coffee at Café La Ventana downstairs?"

"Why not," he said, and followed Sharon out of the room.

Jake removed his hat, pulled a chair away from a wall, and slid it up beside Arthur's bed. Arthur's hand located the push button at the end of the white cord and raised the head of the bed thirty degrees. "Did you find the girls?"

"Right where you said." Jake's eyes bounced around the room. He rested his elbows on his knees and twirled his hat loosely in his fingers. "We scared the hell out of them though. I had a flatbed tow pick up their white Bronco II from the motel, and I've got the girls in protective custody now at the District."

"Did they tell you anything?"

Jake sat up straight, still holding on to his hat, but no longer twirling it. "They left the boys about ten minutes before they were killed. Apparently, they were doing what young boys and girls do at night in places like that. When things got a little bit friskier than the girls liked, they put a stop to it and left. Just to teach them a lesson."

Arthur said, "To pull a stunt like that the girls must have driven them out there and made them think they were leaving them to find their own way home. Did your guys turn up anything knocking on any of those doors around there? Did anyone say they saw or heard anything?" A jolt of pain shot through Arthur's body, taking hold of him momentarily. He hoped whatever painkiller was in the new IV would get going and put a stop to that.

"The girls were going to drive away and come back in about twenty minutes," Jake explained. "They drove off and parked out of sight down the road where that pumpjack is. They turned their lights off and just sat there." Jake paused. "That's when they say they heard a sound they'd never heard before. And they heard it twice. They got scared and high-tailed it outta there, down the road past that metal swing gate, and hid their truck among some junk cars by one of those houses. The resident of one of the houses confirmed they saw a white vehicle, but didn't get a license number, and wasn't too sure what type of vehicle it even was." Jake pointed two spread fingers at his eyes and shook them. "She doesn't see too good."

"I still can't believe they just left the boys."

"They're teenage girls, Arthur," Jake said sympathetically. "They were scared. Anyway, they were parked close enough to the road to see some kind of pickup truck speed by before they left."

"They tell you what kind it was? Get a license number?"

"Like I said, Arthur, they're teenage girls. You'd have a better chance finding out what brand of eye shadow Katy Perry wears than finding out what kind of vehicle it was."

Arthur let out of muffled laugh, which led to a cough that caused his body and head to ache.

"What?" Jake said. "You're surprised I know who Katy Perry is?"

"No," Arthur grinned, shaking his head. "I'm surprised you know anything about eye shadow."

Jake chuckled and said, "Good one," then looked at Arthur more seriously. "They did say the reason the boys may have been targeted was because of what they had seen."

"And what was that?"

"You remember I told you about the guy who was beaten up by a bunch of roughnecks at a gas station?"

Arthur nodded.

"Apparently, the boys not only saw the beating but saw them toss his body into the back of their pickup—you know, the ones they all drive around in with those pennant flags on them. Anyway, the boys had Margaret's old Dodge Diplomat that night and followed the truck from the station. They followed from a safe distance behind, and when they saw the truck pull off onto a dirt road, they killed their lights and used the moonlight to drive by. I checked with the weather service and there was a full moon that night." Jake exhaled. "Long story short, Tsela and Tahoma saw the crew dump the guy's body into a canyon and drive away. I'm guessing, or rather hoping, he was already dead before they threw him over the edge. According to Jennifer and Tiffany, the boys couldn't tell. The boys thought no one had seen them, but someone must have, or they wouldn't be dead now."

Arthur shook his head. The pains in his body had begun to be suppressed by whatever was dripping from the IV, but the aching in his head continued to linger. He reminded himself not to shake it again.

"Could the girls tell you which canyon it was?" Arthur asked.

"Antelope," Jake replied.

"You find the body yet?"

"Nope. But we're still navigating it. It's pretty steep and craggy through there, and the girls couldn't tell us exactly where the body was dumped. I reached out to New Mexico Search and Rescue, and they've got a team moving through the canyon now."

Arthur nodded, then said, "I had a talk with Elias Dayton yesterday afternoon."

Jake's eyes widened a bit and his brow rose slightly. "No shit?"

"Yes, shit. And then I get mysteriously shot at last night on my way home. That tells you right there I'm onto something."

"Could be just a coincidence," Jake said.

"Coincidence, my ass!"

"Calm down, now," Jake warned. "You don't want your heart monitor to start spiking."

"He must have called the shooter after I left," Arthur said. "Someone who knew how to find me." He paused, thinking. "Hell, maybe whoever it was tailed me from the compound?"

Jake shook his head. "I don't see that happening. You're a pretty intuitive fellow. You would have spotted someone on your tail. But, hell, even if it was Dayton, you don't have any proof."

Arthur quickly ran his conversation with Elias Dayton

through his battered mind and located something clinging to his scrambled brain tissue.

"Jake," he said, "whoever you have on it, make sure they go over every inch of my truck. Don't leave anything unchecked."

Jake's face screwed up. "Why? What are you thinking?"

"The only way someone could have known where I was, is if they were tracking me."

"Tracking you?" Jake snorted. "This isn't Europe, and you're sure as hell not Jason Bourne."

"When I was in Dayton's office, he got a call." The hospital room door opened, and Sharon walked back in minus John Sykes in time to hear the last of the conversation. The door closed quietly behind her as she returned to her seat next to her husband's bed. "It sounded like nothing at the time, but after last night, I'd bet he had someone tagging my truck while I was talking with him." Arthur looked at Sharon and smiled, took her hand. "He's running security for NMX, so I bet they have all sorts of high-tech crap they use. Hell, even I could buy a tracking device on the internet for about eighty bucks and track someone using my cell phone."

Arthur noticed Jake glance over at Sharon and smile then stand up and turn his attention back to him. "I'll make sure they loosen every bolt and check behind every piece of insulation. If something's there, we'll find it." Jake frowned and half laughed. "But right now, I've got to get going and deal with a world-class horse thief."

The muscles of Arthur's face pulled up into a smile that made his head throb. "World class, huh?"

"Well, at least decent enough to take off with a fifteen-thousand-dollar quarter horse at the Quick Stop right there on 64. The guy who was transporting the horse pulled in to take a leak and grab some pizza, so he let the horse out to kinda stretch his legs and tied him to the trailer." Jake rested his hands on the bed rails. "Well, while the guy was inside, this kid walks up—we've got him on surveillance video. He unties the horse, and as sweet as you please, starts walking off with him. The guy comes out still gnawing at his pizza slice, sees the kid, drops the pizza, and chases after him. The kid hops on the horse and takes off heading west. He just about knocks over the transport guy as he gallops off, and before you know it, the kid's taking the far turn by the Chat & Chew like Secretariat in the final leg at the Belmont Stakes."

"You get an ID on the kid?" Sharon asked.

"Yeah," Jake answered. "He's a kid named Billy Begay. Because of the video camera at the Quick Stop we got a good look at him. We ran him through the system and found an address." Jake stood up and stretched out his lower back, flexed his hands against the building arthritis pain. "We sent an officer to the house, but the kid's grandmother didn't know anything and claimed she hadn't seen him since the day before. We spoke with some other people in the area who said they saw a kid riding the horse, but no one had any idea where he might have gone." Jake nodded. "We'll find him."

Sharon smiled. "Thanks for everything, Jake."

Jake smiled thoughtfully and walked toward the door of the hospital room, then turned to look back at Arthur. "Let's not make getting shot at a habit, huh?"

Arthur smiled as Jake left the room, leaving Arthur alone with Sharon.

"So, when the hell am I getting out of here?" Arthur said. "Please tell me it's soon."

"I spoke with the doctor while your buddy Sykes and I were having coffee and discussing your military career." She paused to cock her head slightly. "I never knew you were such a player back in the day."

Arthur looked at her from under his bruised brow. "I plead the fifth."

Sharon grinned.

"What other lies did he tell you about me, *Ch'il bilátah hózhóón.*"

Arthur saw his wife's face light up instantly. "You haven't called me *flower* in forever."

"Not since we first started dating," Arthur reminded her, holding her hand as firmly as his bruised and aching body would let him.

Sharon stood up and leaned over him, hovering briefly before kissing him passionately. Arthur winced at first, but her lips and tongue quickly sent a message to his brain that seemed to override the pain in his body. His eyes closed momentarily then opened and watched the green line of his heart rate hop across the screen of the monitor stationed above him. Below it he observed the yellow line representing his blood pressure as it peaked and dove smoothly along the other screen. When Sharon's kiss ended, she sat back down and licked her lips as if she were savoring a forbidden delicacy.

"Damn, you taste good."

"It's the medication. Now, where are my clothes? I want to get the hell out of here."

"Not so fast, Super Indian. Since you have no broken bones, and they've run all their tests for traumatic brain injury and found nothing, you're supposed to be released by three o'clock, which means probably closer to four or five. You're not going anywhere for a few more hours, and then you're going straight home to rest."

"Somebody tried to kill me," Arthur said. "And I'll take all bets at the Northern Edge Casino as to who it was. All I have to do is prove it."

"You're not proving anything to anyone today," Sharon scolded. "You're going home to rest tonight, and that's that." She stood and crossed her arms, a look of determination across her face. "Or do I have to break something to keep you here?"

Sometimes the better part of valor is knowing when to pick your battles, Arthur thought. But he also knew she was right, and given the degree of pain he was feeling, although tempered by the medication, he decided to acquiesce. Even though he had felt far worse in November 2001 when he had been part of the first Marine forces to strike al-Qaeda after the Twin Towers had fallen. *This?* This pain was nothing compared to what he had dealt with when that IED had exploded outside Kandahar. This he could shake off, unlike the ringing in his ears and the shock to his body that day on patrol when others hadn't been so lucky.

Besides, he figured, if the slug that was pulled from the Bronco matched the ones that killed the boys, it meant two things: they were fired by the same person, and whoever it was had missed him intentionally. *But why?* A shooter with that kind of skill could certainly miss if they wanted to, but the chances of missing by accident were extremely slim. They would have had to calculate elevation, windage, humidity, the length of distance, the vehicle's rate of speed, and how far ahead of the target they would have to be to hit the target.

It takes a skilled shooter to miss on purpose.

CHAPTER ELEVEN

Arthur woke slowly but sensed instantly he was not in bed alone. The unmistakable smell of wolf-dog hung in the air, and the heavy extra weight that caused the mattress to sink told him that Ak'is had been keeping a watchful eye on overnight.

Arthur reached out a shaky hand and raked it over the big dog's head, down his thick neck, and over his muscular, furry shoulder. He often found it worked as a tranquilizer for him, the way they say therapy dogs work for seniors and kids in hospitals. He managed to lift his head enough to see Ak'is' golden eyes staring back at him with what appeared to be a worried look. Arthur told him in Diné not to worry. That he was strong. The wolf-dog expelled a deep breath and turned his head into Arthur's petting hand.

Arthur's eyes moved toward the windows of his and Sharon's bedroom, noticing that they had been opened to allow the high-desert breeze to carry in the healing scent of the sage that surrounded their home. He watched as the Creator's breath played with the lace curtains and made them dance. The docking station where his phone charged showed 9:56 a.m. floating in its ocean of incandescent blue. As he cradled his throbbing head back into the pillow, all he could remember was that they had arrived home around six the night before after spending most of the previous day in the hospital after being shot at and surviving the accident the night before that. He remembered Sharon helping him upstairs and her putting him to bed while Ak'is had followed carefully behind. Now it was two hours from noon, almost two days later. *Man*, he thought, *time really flies when you're comatose.*

Ak'is licked his lips twice and continued to watch Arthur from under a thick brow that moved with each new eye position. Arthur could hear the big dog's deep, steady breathing, and it added to the calming effect washing over him. Both of them had just closed their eyes when Sharon entered the bedroom carrying a tray of food and a mug of coffee. Arthur looked at her and smiled. "Wow. Breakfast in bed? I should get hurt more often."

"Ha ha," Sharon remarked playfully. "I suggest you don't, or I'll have to tie you to this bed and keep you as my prisoner."

Arthur struggled to sit himself up and propped his back against the headboard. The pain in his body was definitely still there. His legs hurt, his back ached, and his head still had a residual fog blowing through it that rivaled a London night back when Jack the Ripper ruled.

"As I recall," Arthur joked, "that didn't end well for James Caan."

Ak'is raised his head just enough to sniff the aroma wafting from the tray. Sharon set it on Arthur's nightstand. Not sensing anything appetizing, Ak'is rested his big head back on the bed. Sharon stood with her arms crossed in front of her.

"Don't worry," Sharon said, "I don't know where you keep the sledgehammer." Her grin suddenly took a devious turn. "Although I *would* have you all to myself …" She sat on the edge of the bed and slid a soft hand down his smooth, muscular chest and under the single sheet that covered him. He could feel her fingers searching slowly, the tips of them gently brushing his skin.

"I could do whatever I wanted to you for as long as I wanted ..."

"Do tell," Arthur said. Groggy or not, he wanted to see where this attempt at morning seduction went.

Suddenly, and to his great dismay, she pulled her hand away and readjusted the sheet. "But that's only if I were in the mood. Which I'm not, because you need your rest. I wouldn't want to take advantage of an injured man."

"I wouldn't mind," Arthur said. "Take as much advantage as you like."

Sharon laughed, picked up the tray and placed it on his lap, took one of the napkins and opened it, laid it over his chest. "Just eat your breakfast and shut up. And by the way, mister, why is it I'm always the one cooking for you and you're never cooking for me?"

"That's because I let my fingers do the dialing." Arthur picked up his fork and ate some of the eggs still hot on the plate.

"Well, there are times when a girl likes to be taken care of, you know?"

"I'll make a note." He sipped some coffee.

Sharon feigned frustration and said, "I've got some news for you."

"What kind of news?"

"I had my assistant at the station do some checking on Margaret today, had her go through public records and whatever else she could find."

Arthur swallowed the coffee and replaced it with two bites of thick bacon. "Checking out my old girlfriend, are you?"

Sharon grinned and gave Arthur a wrinkled look. "Not hardly. I just thought I'd follow up with her while you were sleeping."

She sucked on the tip of her middle finger and tapped it against the corner of her husband's mouth, rescuing a crumb of bacon that had clung there. "You don't mind a little help, do you?"

He watched her lips close around the finger and suck off the bacon crumb. He was starting to enjoy breakfast in bed.

"Not at all," he said, still savoring the taste of bacon. Which ranked right up there with his taste for mutton, but not even Sharon could prepare mutton the way his maternal grandmother could, back when she was alive. "What were you hoping to find?"

Sharon slowly, seductively withdrew her finger from her mouth and said, "I wasn't sure, but what she did turn up surprised me."

Arthur ate some more bacon with his eye on the orange juice sitting in the frosted glass. "And what was that?"

Sharon wiped her finger on his napkin. "Did you know that Margaret owns land off of 550?"

Arthur stopped midsip and swallowed. "She never mentioned that to me. Not even when we were kids."

Sharon looked at him quizzically. "Really? Hm. Well, somewhere back around 1874 the allotment processes the government put in motion divided our land and gave Margaret's family forty acres east of Huerfano and south of Angel Peak badlands."

"That seems like a lot of land for the white man to have given an Indian in those days. Are you sure about that?"

"Didn't pay attention much in rez public school, did you?"

Arthur ate some eggs as she explained.

"The provisions of the Dawes Act of 1870 granted the head of a family one hundred and sixty acres, an orphan or person over eighteen years of age eighty acres, and a person under the age of eighteen forty acres. I'm guessing Margaret's family member—probably a male—was under the age of eighteen."

"Like I said, she never mentioned it to me," Arthur said, adding hot sauce to his eggs.

"Probably slipped her foggy memory. Didn't you say she was a *glonnie*?"

"What? No!" Arthur glared at her. "Her life's been ripped apart, Sharon, and she looked for solace in a bottle. Big deal! She's no drunkard. Never has been."

Sharon hesitated, realizing an invisible line had just been crossed, before testing her next question. "You sure you're not looking through the skewed lens of adolescent love?"

Arthur shook his head absently, the thoughts of Margaret and that morning three days ago playing out briefly in his mind. "No. Maybe. I don't know."

"It's okay," Sharon said. "I understand what you mean."

"Do you think there's a way to tie her property to the killings of Tsela and Tahoma? Could NMX have wanted her land badly enough to kill for it?"

"I don't know. But I could do some more digging and see what I come up with."

Arthur drank some coffee. "If we go down that rabbit hole, my guess would be they probably tried to buy her out, or made her an offer to lease, and she refused. Or, if we want to get archaic, they could have seen her as an obstacle and decided to revert back to the tried-and-true Colonial way of acquiring Native lands: by taking away her reasons for not selling."

Sharon said, "That's a wild stretch in today's world."

Arthur's phone broke up the conversation from atop the docking station. Sharon reached over quickly and grabbed it while it continued to ramble through the agonizing xylophone scale. Recognizing the familiar name and number, she tapped the big Accept button.

"*Yá'át'ééh abíní*, Jake," she said.

"I hope I'm not bothering you two this morning," Bilagody said, "but I was hoping to speak with our resident stunt driver."

Sharon smiled. "Hold on." She handed Arthur the phone. "What's up?"

"I wanted to tell you we pulled a latent print off that gum wrapper you found."

"How'd you manage to do that?" Arthur glanced at Sharon.

Jake said, "I figured if we're going to have a chance at solving this before someone else gets killed, we don't have months to wait for a lab—they're overworked and underfunded. I simply decided to go a different route."

"And what route was that?"

"I have this new officer here, Alicia Tom, and she had this crazy idea she could help. She saw me staring at that damn baggie with the wrapper in it the other day and mumbling to myself and told me if I couldn't come up with an answer, maybe she could."

"That's taking a helluva risk with possible evidence."

"Yeah, well, that risk paid off," Jake expressed confidently. "The next day she brought in a small plastic container—the kind you'd put leftovers in—and a bottle of iodine crystals."

Arthur tapped the speaker function on his cell phone so Sharon could hear what Jake was saying. "Iodine crystals?" Arthur repeated.

"She does a lot of backpacking and uses them to purify water. Anyway, she sprinkles some of these crystals in the container and puts the wrapper inside using tweezers from her purse and closes the lid." Jake paused briefly to grab a breath of air before continuing. "Then she went over to the sink and poured some steaming hot water into a pot and floated the container in it."

Arthur could hear the excitement building in the cop's voice, and he smiled at Sharon. She smiled back and said softly, "Girl sure sounds resourceful."

Ak'is still paid them all no mind. He was enjoying relaxing on his parents' bed for a change. He wasn't usually allowed on the giant bed, and he was going to take full advantage of it.

"Arthur, I'll be damned if after a few minutes I couldn't see some vapors floating around inside that container! And after about five minutes, she pulls the container out of the water, dries it off, and opens it. She pulls out your wrapper with the tweezers and lays it on the counter, and I'll be damned again if you couldn't see fingerprints! Kind of a brownish orange, but there they were. Had some pretty good ridge detail, too."

"So you plan to give it to our FBI pal Thorne with prints already developed on it?"

"That's the best part!" Jake said. "The prints were so well formed I had her take digital pictures of them to save them. She said they would probably vanish in a few hours anyway, so by the time I hand them over to the feds, it'll just look like a plain gum wrapper again. But I'm going to tell them what we did and show them the digital photos, give them my findings and explain that the situation called for fast action."

"And you think Thorne will be willing to work with you knowing you tampered with evidence?"

"We'll be just as friendly as the when Democrats and Republicans work together across the aisle." Jake's jovial attitude disappeared quickly. "You're not going to like the result though."

Arthur and Sharon waited.

Finally, Bilagody said, "You sitting down?"

"Better," Arthur said. "I'm laying down."

"When we ran the prints through the system they came back as John Sykes'."

"No way!" Arthur sat upright in bed. Sharon grabbed the tray. Ak'is did nothing. "I don't believe you. Run 'em again!"

"What the hell do you think I did?" Jake countered. "I ran

them three times and got the same result each time. There's no way around it. Sykes is our killer. When I turn the wrapper over to the FBI, the first thing they'll want to do is go out to his place. I've already chosen a liaison officer to go with them."

"Don't get the feds involved yet," Arthur said. "I want a chance to talk to John first. Text me his address."

"That's about the dumbest thing I've ever heard you say," Jake scolded. "What makes you think he won't kill you? He's already tried once. And don't forget someone out there hired him to do it."

"I can't explain it, Jake, but if anyone can talk to him, it'll be me. And we all know who hired him. Elias Dayton."

"I still say you're reaching."

"Look, John's not stupid. If he's our killer, and the feds get there before I have a chance to talk to him, he'll see them coming." Arthur calmed his voice in order to convey his point. "They'll never even hear the shots that kill them."

Arthur heard Jake's heavy breathing as he contemplated his answer. "You've got four hours. Then I call them. I'll send you the address."

CHAPTER TWELVE

Arthur ended the call and tossed the phone onto the bed. "Damnit!"

Sharon sat motionless and said nothing. When she stood, Arthur grabbed the tray from his lap and quickly swung his legs over the side of the bed, his face wincing from the pain. He sat the tray back on the nightstand and stood, then began to pace back and forth. Ak'is raised his head and watched him. Sharon remained silent as Arthur's mind began working through the angles and reasons why one of his own men would try to kill him. And what was Sykes' relationship with the Desert Patriots? Did he believe in all their twisted ideology? Was he part of their security operation? Or was he simply their hired gun?

Arthur stopped pacing. "I have to get out of here. I need to find Sykes and see what he tells me."

"Are you crazy?" Sharon's tone became a mixture of anger and astonishment. "If Jake is right, and he took a shot at you, why would you want to give him another chance?"

"Because he could have killed me and he didn't," Arthur insisted. "You don't know him like I do. He wouldn't have missed. None of us would have missed."

"You're in no shape to go anywhere," Sharon argued. "You just got out of the hospital yesterday."

Arthur went to look for his pants. Sharon took a deep breath and tried to calm herself as she watched her husband wandering the bedroom. "Where are we going?"

"*We* are not going anywhere," Arthur stressed. "*I* am going somewhere."

"And what makes you think that? You're in no condition to drive, and you have no vehicle."

Arthur removed a pair of jeans from behind the small door in his dark wooden dresser where they had been neatly folded and stacked. He tugged them on, pushing past the pain, then began rifling through their closet for a shirt.

"I can drive just fine," he said firmly. "I don't need you with me. I don't want to put you in danger." He managed to get a collared shirt on fairly easily but was fighting with his fumbling motor skills to try to button it up. "If Jake is right, I don't want to risk you getting hurt."

"Me?" Sharon debated. "Look at you! You can't even button your shirt." She moved in front of him and began working each of the buttons into their holes with slender fingers. "I'm going with you, and that's the end of it. And I'm not taking no for an answer."

Ak'is rolled over on the bed and made himself comfortable, front legs limply held aloft while his back legs spread wide, displaying very little inhibition and possibly too much pride.

Arthur said, "Those boys became my responsibility after Eddie died. Don't you get it?" He let Sharon finish buttoning his shirt, then he tucked it into the waistband of his jeans and buckled his leather belt. "It's my job to find out if John is responsible, and if he is, to take care of it."

Sharon crossed her arms, as if manning some invisible blockade between husband and wife, and stared at him, her intentions anchored deeply in her determination. "I'm going with you. I can drive since you don't have your truck and can't even seem to button a shirt."

Arthur raked both hands over his head and tossed his shoulder-blade length black hair behind his back. He searched his wife's face for any hint of an afterthought, any chink in her armor of seriousness. Seeing none, he stood firm. "I'm fine. And you are *not* going."

"You wanna bet?" Sharon's chest inflated and fell. Arthur could tell she was doing all she could to control her anger. "How much pain are you in?"

"Not much."

"Bullshit. I can read it in your lacerated face and battered body. You're not some comic book superhero. You're a man of flesh and bone."

Arthur located his boots and moved as quickly as he could past Sharon to get them. Sitting himself on the end of the bed, he began pulling them on. The pain in his body told him she was right as the first boot slammed home, but his stubbornness fought to hide it from her.

Sharon spun around. "Look, I don't want you to go at all. You need to stay here and rest, *but* if you insist on going, then you're taking me."

"I don't need you getting hurt."

"I. Don't. Care," Sharon snapped. "All I see is a man who lives by some insane moral code constructed inside his stubborn head that puts everyone else's needs above his own. Above *our* own. And I understand that you feel you somehow failed the boys, but you couldn't have protected them from this." Sharon stepped closer to where her husband stood after tugging on his other boot. She brought her hands to Arthur's face and held it as her eyes pleaded with his. "I'm going to drive you, so damn it, let me. I can't lose you. Not now, not ever."

Arthur stood looking at the woman before him. She had been the only one who had been able to reach inside his soul and peel away the many layers of hardened military exterior. An exterior that had kept him alive through five Marine tours and twelve years working for CBP. The only woman he had ever met who could bring out in him the man he always hoped was still inside.

"I'm going to ask you again," Sharon said. "Am I driving you, or are you going to risk your own life behind the wheel?"

Over the last ten years of their marriage, Arthur had become used to finding himself in these types of situations. And he had always felt uncomfortable in them. It reminded him of being in the Marines when they were figuring out strike plans using the ends, ways, means, and risk strategy. He remembered the three-legged stool theory of a plane of varying degrees of risk balancing precariously on top of the three legs representing ends, ways, and means. He quickly calculated the degree of risk regarding this mission and said, "You're driving."

* * *

They had been on the road at least half an hour. Arthur was biding his time, watching the sun move behind the sparsely scattered clouds in the sky as it baked the ground below. His eyes followed the ghostly chemtrails of jets as they crossed over each other and expanded into swaths of disappearing vapor. Sharon was heading south on Highway 550 with the visor of her yellow Toyota FJ Cruiser pulled down to shade her eyes.

"I can't believe I'm riding in this thing," Arthur mumbled from the passenger seat. "I feel like I'm in a pregnant banana on wheels."

"Beggars can't be choosers," Sharon said. "Besides, it'll give us time to talk."

Well, at least she hadn't said, "*We need to talk*," Arthur told him himself. That rarely meant anything good. His gaze returned to staring out of the passenger-side window and admiring the arid scenery as it rolled by. "So they're fracking the hell out of this area, huh?"

Sharon huffed. "If you think DAPL in the Dakotas was a problem, you should really read up on what's going on in Dinétah." Sharon signaled and moved around a slower-moving semi. Arthur hid his face from the driver so as not to be seen in the pregnant banana on wheels.

"Fracking is big business," Sharon added. "So much so that NMX and a few other companies have seen a huge influx in hiring for this region. Especially around Chaco. Did you know there are seventy thousand oil and gas wells in our homeland right now? And the BLM wants to give the okay to double that amount." She shook her head. "That's one hundred and forty thousand needles in the ground, sucking our land dry. Not to mention the thousands of miles of new access roads and plowed pathways for drilling sites. And to top it off, you'll have thousands of miles of pipelines running everywhere." Sharon turned up her side of the air-conditioning to combat the one-hundred-and-two-degree temperature attacking the outside of the SUV as they moved through the sweltering San Juan Basin.

"Doesn't fracking involve pumping liquid into shale deposits?" Arthur said.

"Where'd you hear that?" Sharon said.

"I read an article in the *Navajo Times* about it, 'New Mexico: Land of Extraction,'" Arthur said. "It was a while back, so don't ask me when."

Sharon grinned. "Well, that's pretty much true. The short

version is they pump fluids into shale beds under high pressure so they can extract oil and gas deposits. These fluids are a mixture of water, chemicals, and sand that get injected to reduce friction pressure and create a fracture. The San Juan is loaded with both oil and methane gas deposits."

"But aren't the chemicals dangerous? That seems to be the point of all these yellow protest signs I've been seeing along the road here."

"Depends on which side you talk to. One side tells you all the benefits of fracking while the other side offers you just as many detractions. While it is true that methane gas is a great, nontoxic energy source, the opposition is telling you it's the silent killer everyone should be afraid of." Sharon reached down and jerked her stainless water bottle from the center console and took a drink. "Methane is highly explosive and has been the cause of a lot of mining and rig explosions in the past. But it also comes from humans and cows in, well, the form of farts." She briefly turned her head to look at her husband. "All joking aside, it has been known to cause death by asphyxiation if you're exposed to it for a long enough period of time."

Sharon hit her signal and passed another semi and a sedan with Indiana plates that had slowed down to let someone inside take photos of the passing geologic splendor outside their car window. Another yellow protest sign passed by Arthur's window proclaiming "Extraction or Health and Safety?" in bold black letters.

Arthur turned in his seat. "I also read recently about a young boy who had been run over and killed by an oil-company truck. The paper said the truck was traveling fast on a dirt road that even school buses have trouble navigating."

Sharon lips pursed. "Bottom line is that our people don't feel protected or properly represented. And it's because they don't think they have a voice when it comes to management of federal lands that are next to Tribal Trust lands or any of the allotted lands. And they don't see any transparency pertaining to what's been going on with our local leaders." Sharon shot him a sideways glance. "They're on their own."

Arthur surveyed the round crops of NAPI as they passed them by in the distance. The arrogated crop circles of the Navajo Agricultural Products Industry, if you googled them as he had once, would look like discs of browns and grays and greens, all resembling hundreds of long-playing records if you zoomed in close enough. He remembered hearing about the crops of alfalfa, corn, beans, potatoes, and other smaller grains grown there. He had even used their alfalfa mix for his horses. Sure, sometimes it was dirty, but he figured he was living in the desert so what did he expect?

* * *

Should I tell him now? Sharon wondered. She had only seen the therapist once and had walked out. *Is it even something I should bring up?* Since the medications had worn off, she concluded he did seem fine and normally coherent. He should be able to hold an intelligent conversation. She looked over at him again as he gazed out the passenger-side window toward whatever it was that had captivated his attention in the sparse but rich landscape.

"Have you had a chance to look into that thing I mentioned with your Marine brothers, using social media?" She put the question out there as an icebreaker.

Arthur just shook his head. "Not yet. I've had too many things on my mind." He looked at her. "Especially now."

Arthur returned his gaze out his window to a terrain that was like any other he had seen in his years growing up in this neck of the world. It actually didn't differ that much from anything he had seen during his combat deployment with John Sykes. *Sand is sand*, he thought. *Hard compacted or not. It still soaks up blood.*

"Arthur?" Sharon said.

No response.

"Arthur?" she said again.

He turned his head.

"You okay, babe? You looked like you were a million miles away."

Arthur sat up in his seat, took a deep breath, and let it out through his nostrils. "I was just thinking about John. We'd already had a couple of deployments and were in Iraq at the FOB one night—forward operating base—getting ready to go outside the T-wall again, and this kid who couldn't have been any more than nineteen or twenty was bitching that he'd never had the chance to go out." Arthur could see she was paying close attention while still watching the undulating highway that rolled out in front of her. She always could multitask. "He had a desk job or something and was just aching to see some action."

Sharon said, "T-wall?"

"It's a twelve-foot-high steel-reinforced concrete blast wall that separated us from the bad guys."

Sharon nodded.

"John tells the kid that if he wants to take his slot, he should check and see if it would be allowed. If so, he'd swap with him. Hell, he and I had already been out every day that week." Arthur paused to glance out his window again at the safe world as it passed leisurely by. He let his thumb and forefinger push up his sunglasses, pinch the bridge of this nose. "So the kid goes and gets the okay, and he and I go out the next day with our unit." Arthur's eyes closed. "Long story short, we get hit and the kid gets killed."

"My God."

"That's the kind of shit that happens every day." Arthur paused, his thoughts taking him back momentarily. "Over there you learn quickly to bury everything bad that happens deep inside. You bury it all. Because if you don't, it'll bury you." Arthur adjusted his sunglasses again. "Nevertheless, it becomes ingrained in your memory. Post-deployment you go through some follow-up briefings to try to help you adjust back into normal life when you come home. Then there's counseling and medical evaluations to help you avoid stress in the days afterward. And when we get back discharged, we all try to fit in. Some of us get jobs, go back to our families; some of us go to college, like I did." Arthur snorted a laugh through his nose. "I sat there in a classroom full of a bunch of snowflakes who didn't know a fucking thing about life because their biggest problems were choosing which parties to go to or worrying about how to get laid." He shook his head. "And there I sat … all quiet in the back of the room … a handful of years older than them—and I'd killed people."

Sharon reached a hand over and held his hand in hers. He let their fingers entwine.

"And that's why I don't get it," he said. "How could John go through shit like that and end up being a killer? I just don't buy it."

Sharon didn't look at Arthur when she said what she had already been thinking. She just let it roll off her tongue as if it were water tumbling over a stone. "I guess because the government made him one?"

Arthur looked at her solemnly. "It made us all one."

Sharon ran the thought of telling him about the shrink through her mind again. Maybe he would understand. Maybe he would be supportive. Maybe she should just find that hidden strength Janet Peterson had mentioned and tell him.

Sharon took a deep breath. "I wasn't in a meeting the other day when you called me at the station." There it was. It was out. "I flew to Santa Fe and spoke with a psychiatrist specializing in PTSD."

Arthur turned his head. He saw the anxiety in her body language, her hands gripping the steering wheel hard, the muscles of her jaw clenching and releasing in anticipation of his response. It was the same type of tension he'd felt lying next to her in bed. When he held her close and they snuggled like spoons, he could feel her body tightening briefly, quivering and then relaxing. He had been noticing it more those nights when she struggled to go to sleep. Those nights when the memories came calling. Those nights when the ghosts filled her head.

Sharon said, "You're not mad, are you?"

"Why would I be mad?"

Sharon shook her head. "I don't know."

"Honey, if you need help then by all means seek it out." Suddenly the landscape held no attention for him. All of his focus was on his wife. "How did your first session go?"

Sharon shrugged. "Okay, I guess." She wiped a tear from her eye. "She wanted me to schedule another session, but I told her I wasn't interested."

"If I learned anything from my sessions at Camp Pendleton, it was that I needed to talk about what I went through." He paused. "I think you should go back."

Sharon looked at him. "You do?"

He smiled softly. "Of course. I'll even go with you, if you want me to." He paused. Sharon smiled. He liked that smile. He drank it up like a thirsty plant soaking up a lazy rain. "I've got a confession to make also," he added. "When I was unconscious at the hospital something weird and wonderful happened."

"What?"

He told her of his travels with the holy people through the realms of the four worlds of creation and the spectacles he had witnessed. "I truly believe that my travels were the Creator showing me my path back to you. Because you are my life; you are the river that flows through my soul and gives me purpose."

Suddenly, their world was shattered by the annoying ringtone of Arthur's cell phone. Reluctantly, he pulled it out and answered. "What's up, Jake?"

"New Mexico Search and Rescue found the body Tsela and Tahoma Tabaaha saw being dumped into Antelope Canyon. The family is driving up from Nageezi to identify him." Jake's tone turned somber. "I told them it wasn't necessary, but I didn't tell them why. It's been enough time for the animals and the heat to have taken their toll on the body. Mendoza will probably have to use dental records." Arthur heard the big man sigh. "I think I'm getting tired of this job, my friend. Over twenty-five years of drunks, drugs, car accidents, domestic violence, and murders takes a toll on your soul. I need a cleanse. This walking in two worlds is enough to put you in a rubber room."

Arthur said nothing. He had felt the same way during his twelve years with CBP on the Arizona border. Being brought up Navajo, you were taught that all life is sacred and everything and everyone is connected, that by living the Navajo Way even a Navajo who is not part of your family's clans is to be treated with respect and like they are your family. You learn that everyone across the Navajo Nation is part of your collective family. He said, "Any chance they'll find evidence of the men who did it, to corroborate the girls' stories?"

"Remains to be seen," Jake said. "He was where they said he would be, but it's hearsay because *they* weren't the ones to actually see it happen." Jake paused. "By the way, you were right—a small tracking device was found under your truck.

I have one of my men checking to see where it was sold and to whom."

Arthur looked at Sharon. "That could have only come from one place, Jake, and you know it."

Sharon's face now took on a more serious expression.

"We have to play our cards close on this, Arthur," Jake cautioned. "We need to connect the dots first. Let's make sure we can link the two."

Arthur's face screwed up. "I know it was Elias Dayton. We're on our way to Sykes' place now—"

"We?"

"Sharon insisted on driving. Long story."

"You lost the argument, huh?" Jake chuckled. "Been there, done that. But I don't like that she's with you. Sykes could be a psycho. Anyone who sells their gun always has more than a few screws loose."

"We'll be fine," Arthur insisted.

"Famous last words," Jake said. "Now, listen up, Sykes' woman is named Rosheen Notah, thirty-five years old and works as a cashier at the Stop-N-Go Counselor Post. If your boy isn't there when you get there, then he's left her high and dry to take the heat that's going to come down." Jake breathed heavily. "I'm sure she's oblivious to what's about to happen to her. Poor kid. I can't imagine how she's going to feel being questioned by the Federal Bureau of Inquisition."

"Welcome to being indigenous in the white world," Arthur said. "Sometimes it's like nothing has changed in a hundred years." Arthur thought for a moment. "If we can link John to the Patriots, you and the feds would have probable cause to search Dayton's compound."

"If you come up with something," Jake instructed, "I'd better be the first person you call." Then he added, "I'm going to take a ride out to the Angel Peak Chapter House later this afternoon and listen in on a meeting NMX is holding with the residents."

"Don't they usually do those things in the morning?"

"Normally, yes, but the NMX people already had some corporate crap in the works, so they set it up for later in the day." Jake huffed. "Probably thought the Natives would be too tired to pay attention by then."

"What do you hope to gain there?"

"Like I said, there's supposed to be some company bigwig showing up to convince the people that what they are doing is good for them. Maybe your buddy Dayton will be there with a few of his boys to make sure things flow smoothly. Maybe I can get him to make a mistake in front of the man who writes his checks. At the very least, I'll let him know the law is watching him."

Arthur thanked the police captain and hung up.

Sharon was staring at him, one eye still on the road. "By the look I saw on your face, I'm guessing that wasn't good news?"

Arthur slid the cell into his shirt pocket. "Half and half. They found the body of the man the oil field workers allegedly beat up."

Sharon pursed her lips and slowly shook her head.

"Jake thinks John Sykes may be on the run." He wasn't about to tell her about the tracking device. "Only his woman might be there when we get there."

Sharon's head stopped shaking. "What the hell was he at the hospital for then? To finish the job?"

"I don't think he wanted to kill me," Arthur said. "If he wanted to, I'm sure he could have. I think he wanted to scare me." Arthur grinned. "But I don't scare easy."

CHAPTER THIRTEEN

It was 0600 hours, and the foot patrol had already been on the move for an hour, slowly working through the narrow streets of a town that had already been swept and cleared the week prior. Intelligence had picked up chatter concerning a possible terrorist meeting that was supposed to take place there, so for that reason they had been rousted from their already-limited slumber inside their insulated shipping containers at an ungodly hour, told to grab their gear and be cocked and locked in twenty minutes. Hell, they barely had enough time to brush their teeth at the M-149 Water Buffalo trailer before heading over to be briefed about their mission. Shock and Awe had been deemed a success a few weeks earlier, and now they were being told to pack themselves into three Humvees and disappear into the Iraqi night.

Once on location, however, the whole thing just felt wrong. They were doing a door-to-door and told to keep their eyes wide open and their ears clear. But it was too fucking quiet. Nothing was moving, and the "pucker factor" was way too high; he could feel the small hairs on the back of his neck standing on end and his balls pulling up close to his body. He swallowed the dryness in his mouth and told himself to pull it together. To embrace the suck!

Suddenly, a hailstorm of enemy fire descended upon them.

"Rooftop!" someone yelled. "Get those motherfuckers!"

He returned fire with the rest of his team. The first shots had come from the rooftops. He had seen the muzzle flashes and heard the slugs ripping into the mud walls. Other shots seemed to originate from buildings just up the centuries-old street. Without warning, a fast-moving white Nissan pickup emerged from a side street, fishtailed in the dirt, and headed straight for them. He yelled, "You're gonna die, motherfucker!" and four of his men joined him in firing at the charging pickup, while the rest continued spraying the rooftops. The pickup's windshield spiderwebbed from every round their M4s spat into it. The truck abruptly swerved to its left and crashed into a mud brick wall in front of them. Gunfire continued to buzz past his head, some thudding into the dirt street and some finding their home in the bodies of his comrades who crumpled around him.

Dust from the shattered wall where the pickup had embedded itself now filled the air and mixed with the dust from the street being kicked up by the raining death pounding into it.

"Doorway! Doorway!" someone yelled.

He fired, the unit fired, and the enemy continued to fire. The unit moved forward, keeping close to the wall and using any shelter they could to put a barrier between themselves and the shower of small-arms fire that could easily be carrying any one of their names.

As they approached the pickup, he could see the driver covered in blood and not moving. The engine was still running, the rpms whining high and the radiator steaming like a geyser. Bullets continued to rip into the truck and mud wall around them, sending pieces of each spinning off, stinging their faces and bouncing off their helmets or ricocheting past them like scream-ing death. He glanced into the pickup and saw the driver's right hand loosely holding the trigger meant to set off the car bomb that would have surely killed them all. His chest filled with a sigh of relief as he crouched beside the pickup, but that sensa-tion was short lived. He hadn't noticed the cell phone that had been taped to the bomb, nor did he notice its digital screen light up in the instant it took him to check his men. Within seconds the pickup exploded into a fiery ball with a deafening roar.

The blast threw him thirty feet from the truck to where he lay on the ground, his right arm bleeding, his ears hearing noth-ing but a loud ringing that pierced his clouded brain, and the right side of his face felt like it wasn't even there.

Suddenly, he sat up in bed. The sound of the trailer's air conditioner droning away above him on the roof was the only sound he now heard, aside from that of his own thundering heart. His sweating body shivered as waves of cold air from the unit's AC vents washed over him. He gulped a large swallow of chilled air into his lungs as his chest seemed to heave with a frightened will all its own. He felt a shaky hand move to his throat testing that his Adam's apple was even moving. He could hear himself breathing. It had all been another dream, another nightmare in the endless string of nightmares that he had been forced to live through since he had gotten back home.

It took him a long string of minutes to recognize his surroundings and bring them into focus. The cheap curtains that covered the sun-yellowed roller shades on the windows were doing their best to keep the afternoon sun out of his eyes. He rolled over under the wet sheets and tossed them off, swung his legs over the edge of the bed and sat there, letting the soles of his feet appreciate the low pile of the carpeted floor. His body felt clammy and his mind raced. He felt tired and drained—tired of the nightmares that seemed to change nightly, tired of the deafening sounds that constantly haunted his darkened mind, and tired of the demons that beckoned him always.

Tears welled up in his eyes from out of nowhere, and suddenly his body began to shake as he cried uncontrollably. Holding his face in his hands, his shoulders rocked with every sob that shook his core. Wiping the salty streams of pain from his stubbled face, he reached under his pillow and wrapped his fingers around the comfortable grip of the Colt Combat Commander 9 mm semiautomatic he kept there. He pulled her out and studied her in his hand, his palm feeling her loaded weight and smelling the oil that lubricated her mechanisms.

I can't do this anymore, his own voice echoed inside his head. *I can't live like this. Maybe the others were right. This is the only way to make it stop.*

He watched his thumb disengage the safety. He felt his palm push in the grip safety as his hand tightened around the checkered black cherrywood grips. His chest filled with a deep breath—his last breath—as he put the carbon blued steel muzzle of the semiautomatic to his forehead, his thumb rested on the curved three-holed trigger. His anxiety level rose exponentially, and he swore he could feel his own heart pounding in his throat.

Just five pounds of trigger pull and it will all be over. You can do this! Don't fucking bail, you fucking coward! He brought his left hand up to steady the weapon and pressed the muzzle harder into his forehead. He needed to make sure it could complete its final task.

"C'mon, asshole, finish it!" his voice raged out loud. "Fucking finish it!"

He closed his eyes tightly and pulled the trigger.

Nothing.

The weapon hadn't fired. The hammer had fallen and then

nothing, not a goddamned sound except the hammer striking home and that fucking air conditioner. His breathing shuddered and his hands trembled as he opened his eyes. Staring down at his own fingers curled around the pistol, he wondered why his brains weren't splattered all over the wall behind him, why this gun wasn't laying on the carpeted floor for someone, anyone, to find when they came to check on him. And why there wasn't a small, black hole in the center of his forehead and a larger, fist-sized hole out the back.

He let the dead weight of his hands fall to his lap as he continued to stare at the semiautomatic. Raising it up again, he let the fingers of his left hand push back the slide. He watched as the shell ejected and tumbled effortlessly in the air in what seemed like a slow-motion scene from a Sam Peckinpah film and land on the wet fitted sheet of the bed.

He picked it up and studied its brass casing. The hollow point tip was still intact. It was a dud. A fucking dud! Even the manufacturer couldn't get it right.

He set the bullet on the nightstand and stared at it. It stood there, mocking him, taunting him with the promise of the release he so desperately wanted, but couldn't have. He tossed the Colt onto the bed and fisted his cell phone, chose the banking app and checked his bank account to make sure Dayton's deposit had arrived. It had. His job for tonight had been paid in full.

CHAPTER FOURTEEN

Jake Bilagody's hands had been fighting him since the moment he had gotten out of bed that morning. The arthritis attacking the fingers of his left hand had swollen them up to the point where he was thankful he no longer wore a wedding band. Initially, that fact had been depressing for him to deal with, but he had slowly come to terms with it over the last few years. If one ever really did come to terms with it. He sat behind the desk in his office and held his hands out in front of him, palms up. He tried to curl his fingers toward his palm and rest his thumbs over them, but he couldn't.

With each attempt, the big man cringed in pain. The joints of his fingers felt like they were bone grinding on bone. He stared at them now with deepening regret, remembering how he had never listened to any of the elders who had always advised him against popping his knuckles. Now that arrogance had seemingly come back to haunt him in the pregolden years known as middle age. For a moment, he stared at the spot where his wedding ring would have resided. Maybe he should try calling his ex-wife? The thought had run through his mind several times in recent days. Nizhoni, which meant *beautiful* in Navajo, hadn't bothered to contact him after the divorce, apparently moving on without giving their marriage a second thought. *Twenty-five years together and I guess it meant nothing.* Jake inhaled deeply and let his breath escape, taking his thought along with it.

He pulled open the top left-hand drawer of his desk and removed a small jar of arthritis cream, twisted off the lid, and set it top down on his blotter. Dipping the index and middle finger of his right hand into the container, he removed a daub of cream and set the jar on the desk next to the lid. Massaging the cream into the joints of his left hand, he focused on the night ahead of him. Currently it was the Tuba City district captain's task to fill the vacant seat left by the abdicating chief in Window Rock. Another year of this round-robin crap, and he'd have to think of abdicating himself. This was the second year without an actual leader, and the division captains were still taking up the slack. The first year had been rough. But now, after the long commutes, the late nights, and the early mornings, he was somewhat used to it, even at his age. The teenage horse thief had been apprehended and was now resting in a cell, awaiting arraignment. The transport driver had taken up residence in one of the local motels until the horse could be loaded up, and he could be on his way. Outside of that, it had been a slow day, and Jake was glad of it.

A knock on the doorjamb of his office rattled the captain's concentration. He lifted his head to see Officer Brandon Descheene standing in his doorway, grinning sheepishly.

"What are you looking at?" Jake barked at the twenty-seven-year-old. "I've even got a plastic pill container at home with the days of the week on it." Jake massaged the white cream into the tissue of his left hand until it vanished. "Wait till you get old, kid. It's all fun and games now, but you just wait."

Officer Descheene stepped into the office and stood in front of the desk. "I just came back from patrol with a DUI," he said, hesitating. "I put her in holding until you decided what you wanted to do with her."

Bilagody screwed the lid back on the jar and returned it to the upper left-hand drawer. "Did you file any paperwork?"

"No, sir. I literally just got back about ten minutes ago. As I said, I wanted to see what you wanted to do first."

Jake's face twisted in confusion at the statement. "And why is that? Don't tell me it's that singer from the Dancing Water Casino again?" He shook his head. "That woman couldn't hold her liquor if you glued the glass to her hand."

Officer Brandon Descheene looked embarrassed, although not for himself, and glanced at his shoes again so his eyes wouldn't meet with his captain's. "No, sir," he said. "It's Margaret Tabaaha."

* * *

Captain Jake Bilagody opened the door of Interrogation Room One. He had removed his sidearm and given it to Descheene even though he knew there was no real threat. It was procedure to do so, and what type of example would he be to his officers if he ignored procedure. Margaret Tabaaha sat slumped over and sleeping on the bare table in front of the mirrored two-way glass, her head resting on her crossed arms like a kindergartener at nap time. Her hair, a black unwashed mess, lay covering most of her back and her left arm like a large Chinese paper fan that had been opened before she had fallen asleep.

Bilagody noticed her dingy white shirt, dirty jeans, and the equally soiled gym shoes that offset the sanitized feel of the small room. And judging by the aroma wafting from her pores, she hadn't bathed or changed her clothes since he had last seen her at Flat Iron Rock. He closed the door quietly behind him and stepped over to her. Her breathing was relaxed by sleep and her breaths were being doled out in long, evenly measured doses by her drunken state.

Jake reached out a cautious hand and gently jostled her left shoulder. "Margaret?"

No response.

He jostled her again. "*Atsi'*," he said softly, calling her *daughter* in their Native language, as most elders would, even if the person they were speaking to was not directly related to them.

Again, there was no real response, just a soft sigh and a slight movement of a foot. Jake nudged her shoulder with the back of his large hand this time and raised his baritone voice. "Hey! Wake up!"

"Fuck you!" she grunted, slapping his hand away as she pushed herself into a lazy sitting position. "What you doing? Leave me alone, *hágoshįį'?*"

Jake smiled because she had used a Navajo word at the end of an English sentence. "At least you have not forgotten how to speak Diné, drunk or not."

Jake could tell she was having trouble focusing her glazed eyes because it was taking her too long to respond. "I can remember a lot more words that just *okay* in Diné," she chided. "*Téliicho'í!*"

Jake laughed, and when he did—which seemed to be only on rare occasions these days—his belly shook noticeably. "I've been called a lot worse than jackass in my time," he said as he reached out and tugged a metal chair away from the other side of the table. He sat his large frame down in front of her. "Margaret," he began sympathetically. "Do you know why you were brought here?"

Her head tilted back and wobbled a bit as she focused on the question. "Cause your boy picked me up."

"That's right."

"I was jus' going home, eh? I wasn't doin' nothin'." Margaret's head leaned forward as if to doze off, then snapped back. "You can't keep me here, ya know?" A drunken thumb pointed at her chest. "I have rights."

Jake rubbed his face and took a breath, four fingers covering his mouth, thumb resting against his cheekbone. His lips tasted the lingering arthritis cream, and he quickly pulled his hand away from his face and wiped his lips on his shirt sleeve.

By the way she was slurring and her condition of dress, Jake knew her blood alcohol level was surely above the .08 percent limit for operating a motor vehicle. Of that there was no question. But there were extenuating circumstances here, ones that some, if not most people with a conscience and a moral compass would understand. But would they understand what he was about to do? It was a good thing he was one of the acting chiefs of police with the Navajo Department of Public Safety. He closed his eyes briefly and wished he had his ceremonial pipe. He could offer his prayers in the smoke and let the smoke take his prayers to the Creator. *Hódzą́ shiih nílé.* Give me wisdom.

"Actually, Margaret, I *can* hold you here … and for as long as I need to." He watched her stare at him through inebriated eyes, then added, "I think that for tonight, I'm going to keep you safe."

She scoffed and belched an invisible cloud that almost gagged him, then paused for a moment as if to let her dull eyes settle on a distant memory. "My boys are dead," she mumbled. "They won' be comin' home no more. My husband's dead, too." She exhaled sorrowfully. "I have nothing."

"Listen to me, Margaret. Margaret, listen to me," he repeated calmly. "I'm going to keep you here until tomorrow so you can sober up. And when your head is clear, I'll have them bring you in some food and coffee, and we're going to have a little talk." He nodded his head for her to see. "Wouldn't that be nice? After that, you can go home." He held her face up with his half-curled fingers. "Okay?"

Before she could muster an answer, her eyes fell shut and her body went limp. Jake was in the process of catching her as Officer Descheene entered the interrogation room. He rushed forward and took her dead weight from Jake.

"Let's get her to a quiet place to sleep it off."

Officer Descheene nodded.

"You were right," Jake said. "Forget about that report. And have her car towed to the station so she can get back home tomorrow. I'll pay for it. And make sure she gets breakfast in the morning."

Officer Brandon Descheene nodded again. Jake instructed him to lift her feet and open the door. He put his big arms under hers and carried most of her weight, and the three of them left the room quietly.

CHAPTER FIFTEEN

Jake had been right. The weathered single-wide trailer of Rosheen Notah sat on the left side of the road across from the spectacle that was the Black Mounds of the Navajo Nation. Its robin-egg-blue color had faded over the years into an almost white, which contrasted well against the remarkable layers of sandstone, shale, and coal that had been so artfully and precisely fashioned over the past sixty-five million years. The tops of the rounded mounds were covered by a thick layer of caprock that gave the badlands-designated wilderness area an eerie blackish-gray lunar landscape that reminded him of the Lybrook formations farther south, only on a smaller scale.

The pregnant banana on wheels took the rutted dirt exit that veered off to the left at a forty-five-degree angle from the graded road. It bounced along the uneven stretch that led to the trailer and quickly rolled to a stop. Sharon and Arthur both noticed the bank of angled solar panels lining the rooftop, soaking up the sun's energy as it moved across Father Sky. They glanced at each other before getting out and feeling the heat of the late afternoon baking them in their clothes. The slight breeze that blew across the barren land did little to cool their skin. Arthur could tell by the rain clouds moving in from the southwest that at least the rain held the promise of cooler temperatures, however briefly they might last. The winds would blow, the loose sands would shift, and the ancestors would visit in the form of the water that would fall from the sky and fill the dry creek beds and washes. Arthur had always envisioned them as persistent evolutionary craftsman that continued to carve their way through the landscape like an army of woodworkers' chisels, each one further deepening the grooves and crevices already created by the ancient ones.

Sharon said, "Well, we didn't get shot at, so that's a plus."

"Looks like no one's home."

"Jake said he had a woman, right?"

"Yeah," Arthur replied. "Maybe she's at work. I don't see a vehicle." He looked down at the crisscrossing tracks in the sand at his feet and on the ground around them then squatted down for a closer look. "I make out two vehicles from the tread patterns. One's a wide-lug off-road tire and the other is a regular light-truck all-terrain tire. Both of them head off the way we came."

"I love it when you talk rubber," Sharon quipped.

Arthur laughed as he walked up to the door of the trailer and tried the knob. Locked. Sharon walked up to a middle window. With the trailer resting on wheels and cinder blocks for stability, the window was just out of reach.

"Lift me up so I can see in," she said.

Arthur walked over and squatted down, wrapped his aching arms around her thighs, and lifted her into the air on throbbing legs. The pain of his bruised thighs and battered shins telegraphed they couldn't hold their position for long, even as she alternated from hand to hand like a shovel-snouted lizard on the hot aluminum facade and peered into the trailer. Arthur felt the weight of his wife in his biceps as he nuzzled the left side of his face comfortably against her behind.

"Don't see anyone inside," Sharon reported, "and nothing out of the ordinary either—living room-kitchen combo with, I'm guessing, a master bedroom in the back and a smaller one up front. You can put me down now."

"Not sure I want to," Arthur said confidently. "I kinda like where my head is right now. Feels all nice and cozy."

Sharon slapped the top of his head playfully. "Put me down, you fool. My hands can't take much more of this aluminum."

Reluctantly, Arthur squatted and placed her gently back on the ground. She spun quickly, lazily wrapping her arms around his neck. "You liked that, huh?"

"Very much so," he grinned.

Sharon kissed his mouth briefly. "Ha! Bet you did!"

As they separated, the growling engine of a vehicle could be heard approaching from behind. They turned as a faded mint-green 1980s Ford pickup came charging up the small incline toward the ridge where the trailer was stationed. Arthur couldn't tell who the driver was; however, the law of probabilities dictated it was most likely Rosheen Notah.

They both watched the truck skid to a dusty stop about twenty feet from them. Arthur made note of the N8VGAL front license plate. The woman behind the wheel stared at them suspiciously, possibly determining whether she should take the risk of getting out or cranking the wheel hard to the right and punching the gas. She made her decision and, to Arthur's surprise, turned off the engine.

When she climbed out of the truck, Arthur noticed the tight jeans and a light-blue tank top that showed off the tattoos on both of her arms, while a pair of well-worn cowboy boots seemed at home wearing the soil of the Land of Enchantment.

Her hair was ebony and almost as long as Sharon's. It seemed as though she had paid heed to her elders when she was a little girl about not cutting her hair. It was told, Arthur remembered, that the heavy rains that came across the parched land represented one's hair. And if one didn't cut one's hair then one would always have rain for their crops and animals. But if you disobeyed and cut your hair, the rain's blessings would vanish along with your locks and your animals and crops would starve.

"Who the hell are you two?" the woman asked.

"I'm Arthur Nakai, and this is my wife, Sharon. Are you Rosheen Notah?"

The woman nodded. "Nakai?" Rosheen said. "John often spoke of you. He always called you a friend." She noticed his bruised hands and lacerated face. "What happened to you?"

"Can we go inside?" he suggested. "We need to talk about John."

"Sure. I figured you'd be around some time."

She walked between them, keys in hand, and took the few steps up to the locked door of the trailer. Once unlocked, they followed her inside. The inside was just as hot as the outside. It felt like they had walked into an oven. Rosheen moved to a window-unit air conditioner and switched it on high. Arthur could feel the unit working hard as it geared up to fill the room and then the trailer with refrigerated air.

Rosheen Notah said, "Solar panels can only do so much. John bought us a 5000 BTU unit, so it would cool this place down quickly. I can't leave the AC on all day while I'm gone or I'll have no power in the cells for anything else. You two want something to drink?"

"Water would be good," Sharon said. Arthur agreed.

Rosheen opened the small fridge in the kitchen, pulled out two bottles of water and doled them out, then pulled one for herself and sat on the tattered sofa against the wall opposite of the living room. She propped her feet up on the second-hand coffee table, boots and all. Sharon and Arthur sat in two armchairs that matched the sofa's dull cloth pattern and faced it at right and left angles. Arthur's eyes ran over the cluster of photographs on the wall above the sofa where Rosheen sat. They ranged from happy pictures of her and John Sykes to what appeared to be family photos to photos of John looking proud at the back of his Dodge pickup, an array of rifles laid out on the gray bedrug, to photos of his Marine unit back in the day. Arthur also noticed there was no TV in the main room, just a radio on the kitchen counter. Out here you either had satellite, if you could afford it, or nothing at all. And knowing John, Arthur figured, there wasn't any need for it.

There was an awkward silence among the three of them until Rosheen Notah asked about Arthur's face again.

"Your boyfriend shot at my husband," Sharon stated flatly. "He almost killed him."

"Bullshit!" Rosheen said. "You two were like brothers. He told me so. He would never have done that."

Arthur said, "So John wasn't here last night?"

"No."

"Do you know where he was three nights ago?" Arthur asked calmly, unscrewing the cap on his bottle before taking a drink.

"I don't know," Rosheen said. "When I got home from work, he wasn't here. But that's not unusual. Oftentimes he gets home after I do, so I didn't think anything of it. But when he didn't get home by ten o'clock, I called him."

"What did he say?"

"He didn't answer. Phone went straight to voicemail. I got tired of waiting, so I put a plate of food in the fridge for him and went to bed. He woke me up when he got home—"

"What time was that?" Arthur interrupted.

"Around two or three, I think. I asked him where he'd been. He said he was out night shooting. He'd just bought a new scope or something and was trying it out. Yesterday I came home from work and noticed that some of his stuff was gone. I haven't heard from him since. But I still don't believe John took a shot at you."

"The police seem pretty sure," Arthur countered. "The bullets they dug out of my truck match the ones used to the kill two boys at Flat Iron Rock three nights ago." He waited for her reaction. Nothing. "And they found his fingerprints at the murder scene." Arthur watched her eyes widen slightly at that revelation, her mind tumbling through thoughts he could only imagine.

"I don't want to believe you, but it's looking like I have no other choice."

Rosheen Notah got up and removed a framed photograph from the wall that Arthur had been staring at, walked across the floor to Arthur and handed it to him. Arthur took the photograph and looked at it.

"I remember the day this was taken," he said. "Opening weeks of Operation Enduring Freedom."

"I bet there's a story," Sharon said.

"Our base camp had been set up in an airport southwest of Mosul in Iraq. We had a Fobbit take this pic of us before we went to the mess tent."

"Fobbit?" Sharon said.

"A soldier that never leaves the forward operating base," Rosheen blurted out.

Arthur smiled. Sharon looked at her.

Arthur's eyes never left the photograph, remembering every detail of that day. "Twenty minutes after this was taken, some Haji blew himself up with a suicide bomb he'd smuggled into the tent in a cooler and everything turned to shit." He sighed. "It sucks when no one outside the gate wants you there."

Sharon's hand went to her mouth. Rosheen simply sipped her water. She had obviously heard this story before.

Arthur tapped the photo on his leg and held it back out for Rosheen Notah to retrieve. She did and returned it to its place on the wall above the sofa.

"Nineteen US soldiers were killed that day," Arthur said. "Along with some Iraqi National Guard, a few civilians, and some contractor employees, around sixty or so altogether." Arthur paused, reflecting. Reliving. "I remember the blood all over the concrete floor, making it slippery for those of us who were trying to get the injured away from the melting chairs and tables. Some had parts of them stuck to their skin, so we just stretchered everything, chair and all."

Sharon grimaced. Arthur saw tears trickling from her eyes and running down her face. Rosheen still sat there, motionless, unaffected, sipping her water.

"Forgive me," Arthur said. "It's just that it's all still fresh in my mind … even though it was almost twenty years ago."

Sharon composed herself and tapped into her reporter's alter ego. "Surely you have an idea of where John might go," she prodded. "You've been with him how long?"

"Five years." Her eyes told Sharon she was lost in thought, flipping through the pages of her scrapbook memory. "He had this one place where he would go and practice. Sometimes a couple of his friends would meet him there."

"Practice what?" Sharon said, unscrewing the cap from her bottle and taking small sips.

"His shooting," Rosheen said. "He would go there every now and then and practice shooting. Like that night with the scope. I just figured it was one of those macho guy things, or he needed somewhere to think and get away from me for a while."

"Who would go out there with him?" Arthur said.

"Like I said, a few of his friends. I never met them. That is to say, he never brought them by here, so ..."

"Guys from his old unit?" Sharon asked.

Rosheen opened her bottle and took a mouthful of water. Swallowed. "I don't know. Maybe? I don't know. Like I said, I never met them. All I know is that John needed to go off somewhere and play with his guns. I don't like guns and didn't allow him to have them in the house, so he kept them hidden somewhere. Some he kept in his truck—his rifle and a handgun—the rest in a storage locker he rented somewhere." She hung her head slightly. "I guess he played me for a fool."

Rosheen Notah pulled her feet to the edge of the coffee table, keeping her knees together. She kept the water bottle in her hands on her lap. Her move gave Arthur a chance to study the soles of her boots. The usual scuffs, leftover dirt, and some minute bits of gravel could be seen in the leather sole, but not much else that told him anything.

Arthur let his eyes move to her face. It was smooth, except for the lip ring hooked into the left corner of her mouth. And, based on the photographs arranged along with the others on the wall, she definitely showed some of the features from her mother's side. Also arranged among the family portraits were a few small photos of her and John Sykes taken in places that looked hard to get to except by hiking. One even seemed to be taken where John practiced at his makeshift shooting range. Arthur saw a folding table set up with all the paraphernalia needed for range shooting. There was one where he and Rosheen were smiling and standing next to each other, arms wrapped around each other and sporting broad smiles against the passenger side of an old Dodge Power Wagon. The truck was yellow with a black hood and black strips along the rocker panels. A single yellow roll bar stood behind the standard cab. Next to it was another photograph showing the bed of the truck, tailgate down with John's rifles, ammo, and handguns laid out on the carpeted tailgate of the bedrug.

Arthur nodded, looked at Sharon. "Did he leave any of his things here? Is there anything of yours that you noticed was missing?"

"No, nothing's missing," she said. "And the only things he left were some clothes and his books."

Arthur's eyes passed from his wife's back to Notah. "You think I could take a look around?"

Notah finished her bottle of water, crushed it, and screwed the cap back on. "Sure. It's not like he's gonna be coming back for any of it."

Sharon could feel the weight of that thought blanketing Rosheen Notah's face. Disappointment in men seemed to be rite of passage for a lot of women on the rez. If they didn't beat you or cheat on you, they up and left with no reason given or implied and never returned. Or they simply had no job and no prospects and just used you until they became someone else's problem. But at least she hadn't been a side chick.

Sharon said, "May I use your bathroom?"

Rosheen Notah set her crushed water bottle on the coffee table and stood. "Sure." She pointed past Arthur toward a short hallway to the right of the kitchen. "Master bedroom is through that door. Have a field day."

Arthur watched as Rosheen led Sharon down the other hallway toward the front of the trailer and the front bedroom. He stepped up to the sofa to get a closer look at the photo of the truck with the tailgate down. A small grin curled his mouth when he noticed the yellow bumper sticker clinging to the rear window behind the driver's seat that said "US Marine— We don't suffer from insanity. We enjoy it daily." Arthur's grin quickly faded as he turned and made his way past the kitchen. He noticed a louvered door on his left, which he figured housed the furnace and water heater, and the side rear-entry door of the trailer on his right before entering the master bedroom.

The first thing Arthur noticed was that Rosheen Notah was like Sharon, a fanatic when it came to a made bed. It was as precise as it could be and showed the skill of clean lines and sharp corners. He didn't have any change or he would have bounced a quarter on it. He moved into the room and went straight to the walk-in closet, rummaging through the pockets of John's remaining clothing that hung on wooden hangers. Rosheen's clothes hung on multicolored plastic hangers of varying thicknesses. It looked like John hadn't taken very many clothes, probably only a handful in a duffle along with whatever else a man on the run would need.

It was a given, Arthur supposed, that John would have weapons and ammunition along with some clothes and a decent amount of cash, since credit cards would be a perfect way to track his movements and would now be out of the question. If he could only find out where the hell Sykes was going, this whole thing could almost be over, and he could tell Margaret he had found the man who had taken the lives of her sons. He was sure that right now Jake Bilagody and the FBI had no clue where to look for John, but at least the FBI could ping his cell phone once they got involved. Unless he had already tossed it out and replaced it with a burner phone. At the very least, they could have every cop in the basin looking for his yellow pickup. After all, how many bumblebee-colored 1980 Dodge Power Wagons could there be in the basin?

Arthur searched every shoe, every boot, and every box

that took up space in the closet before moving to the tall, narrow lingerie chest between the two windows that faced the bed and gave the room light. It was a cheap one, obviously purchased at one of those big-box stores and made out of assembled particleboard and laminated cardboard. He felt a bit awkward letting his fingers rifle freely through another woman's underwear. He relaxed when Sharon entered the room and caught him in the act.

"You never told me you had a fetish for ladies' panties," she said with an impish grin.

Arthur turned, eyebrow raised. "Only yours. Why don't you look through this stuff while I hit the dresser?"

"Sure thing, Sherlock." She stepped up to take his place. "What am I looking for?"

"Anything that shouldn't be in there."

The wide dresser was stationed to the left of the bathroom door in the center of the back wall. From the doorway, he could see the double sinks of the contractor-grade vanity, the mirror above it reflecting the opposite wall, and the five baseball-sized frosted glass bulbs above that. To the right of the double sink was the toilet, to the left a shower-tub combination partially hidden by the brown shower curtain sporting a row of stampeding stallions splashing though the water of a shallow river.

He turned his attention to the dresser as Rosheen Notah entered the bedroom and sat on the end of the bed, wrinkling the pristine sheets. "I don't know what you two think you're going to find," she said. "But you're probably not going to find it in my lingerie chest."

Sharon turned and smiled but kept working her way down, one small panty-filled drawer at a time.

Arthur had finished rummaging through the two top drawers of the dresser and pulled open the second set before responding. "You never know what you might find until you find it. Whatever *it* may be."

Sharon was squatting now, being careful not to mess up the arrangement of the contents of the bottom drawer. Finding nothing of any interest, she stood and watched her husband search the two bottom drawers of the dresser. Sharon walked over to the bed and stood next to Rosheen Notah while Arthur closed the drawers and crossed over to a bookcase to the right of the walk-in closet door.

"I remember when Arthur and I first met," Sharon said with a smile. "It was at Chaco." Rosheen looked up at her briefly and smiled back. "Where did you and John meet?"

Rosheen put her arms behind her like a bipod and supported herself on the mattress. Her hair dusted the top of the bed. "He pulled in where I work, for gas and to use the bathroom. We only have one, and it's a small one. He went to open the door and there was this old Navajo woman, an elder, in there." Rosheen giggled. "He looked so embarrassed. The door doesn't lock very well, so it just kind of happened."

"Oh my," Sharon agreed. "That must have been a sight."

Arthur began pulling out each of the books from the shelves, starting with the tattered Tony Hillerman novel on the top shelf. He then proceeded to work through each book quickly, moving left to right through the shelf.

"It was all I could do to keep from laughing out loud," Rosheen remarked. "Then, to pass the time while waiting for the old woman to come out, he wandered around the store checking out the ice-cream cooler and looking into the back room and the loading area. He even stood and admired our little post office boxes mounted on the wall by the bathroom."

Arthur moved on to the second shelf, grabbing each book as he had on the previous shelf, and fanning through their pages with his thumb before returning the book and grabbing another. "What did the old woman do when she came out?" Sharon asked.

Rosheen giggled again. "She looked around to see if he was still in the store, then made sure she walked a wide distance around him." Her head cocked playfully to the left. "I bet it was the first time a man had seen her with her pants down since 1968!"

As the two women laughed, Arthur moved on to the next shelf and pulled out a Craig Johnson novel and fanned through it. Then another. And another. And another.

"Life was good for a while," Rosheen added. "John used to be fun. Sure, he had an ex-wife and a kid, but who doesn't have baggage after a certain age, you know? I mean, face it, the male gene pool—especially on the rez—gets pretty shallow after a while, so you have to take what you can get sometimes, right?" Her eyebrows arched, and she half smiled. "I've had my share of rez men smelling like alcohol, weed, and lies. But John was something different, you know?"

Sharon noticed a tear build up in the corner of Notah's eye and watched her hand absently wipe it away. Arthur turned to look then went back to his work.

Sharon said, "What happened?"

"He changed."

Sharon sat next to her on the bed and spoke to her like a friend, a sister even. Arthur had seen her do it before. Not simply because she had learned to have empathy from her years as a reporter, but because that emotion was indelibly carved into her being. "How did he change?"

Rosheen sat on her hands now, her tattooed arms tucked in close to her sides. "There were nights he would have nightmares and night sweats, you know, and he would wake up scream-ing." She paused to sniffle and control her welling emotions.

"Then there were nights I would see him sitting outside by the firepit, and all he would do is stare into the flames ... like he was lost inside them, you know?" She looked at Sharon. "Like he was seeing some kind of vision in them."

Arthur had been listening as she spoke and could relate to the girl's story. In his first days stateside, right after his time in the Marines had ended, he too had often found himself lost, reliving a part of his past he could never outrun. He removed a copy of *American Indian Trickster Tales* and opened its yellowish cover. Instantly, a small scrap of paper tumbled to the floor by his feet. His eyes dropped to it, and he squatted down, pinching it between the thumb and forefinger of his right hand. He stood and placed the book back into its slot on the shelf and opened the piece of paper.

He stared silently at the scribbling on the paper until he felt the presence of both Sharon and Rosheen Notah lurking behind him. Flanking him, they looked down at the two strings of numbers on the small unfolded paper in Arthur's hands and said nothing.

One string was a set of nine digits, the other a string of eight.

"Are those phone numbers?" Rosheen said. "If that fucker was cheating on me, I—"

"Phone numbers have seven or ten digits," Sharon remarked. "These could be a combination or something?"

"I don't think so," Arthur said. "Most combinations work from zero to ninety-nine. This is something I haven't seen in a long time."

"What are they then?" Rosheen asked.

He looked at her, then at his wife. "I'm willing to bet they're coordinates."

Sharon said, "Coordinates for what?"

"Not what," Arthur answered. "Where."

CHAPTER SIXTEEN

The angled blue metal roof and white adobe walls of the Angel Peak chapter house sat on an area of land encircled by a tall chain-link fence that the local residents referred to as *the compound.* It occupied an area where two BIA graded roads met before sloping downhill slightly and disappearing off into the desert toward the east and Highway 550. To the right of the main building sat the youth and senior citizen centers, both of which were often used as the community hub for potluck suppers, free lunches, and celebrations, along with a flurry of voting activities during election days.

Jake Bilagody rested himself against the left wall of the open hall used for chapter meetings and, as was the case today, a listening session to talk about NMX and its drilling and fracking practices on Dinétah, the Navajo homeland. The late afternoon sun funneling through the square-paned windows that ran around the hall cast its golden light on the rows of plastic folding chairs set up for the expected masses. Jake watched the chairs fill with residents who had come to listen to what the oil and gas company officials had to say, even though most of them had already made up their minds and had come ready for a fight. Jake could see it in their eyes, their demeanor. He had learned early in his career how to read people and what he saw in many of his fellow Diné were building tensions concerning the land, the water, and their health—not necessarily in that order.

A small group of environmental activists filed their way in, along with some stragglers from the parking lot, and found a spot against the opposite wall and waited, poster-board signs and chanting lungs at the ready. Jake was pleased to see that some of the younger people—younger than he was at least—had given up their seats to their elders so they could sit comfortably during the meeting. Soon four members of the Navajo Nation Council walked in and took their respective seats behind their folded-paper nameplates resting on the two six-foot-long plastic folding tables at the front of the large hall.

Behind them rose the dais, which stood less than two feet off the floor and was hidden behind a faux stone partition with pictures of the current Navajo Nation president and other officials decorating the wall behind it on both sides of the large white dry-erase board. To their left, the star-spangled banner hung proudly along with the Navajo Nation and the New Mexico flags. The speaker opened up the session by reminding everyone of the rules that would apply to the afternoon's discussion. When he was confident the crowd had understood, he introduced the official from NMX and asked him to join them.

Jake studied the apprehensive and agitated crowd as a tall, gray-haired man in a crisp white shirt and impeccably tailored gray suit entered the room through a set of double doors across from him and next to the environmental activists. He could see the crowd's contempt for the man before he had even said a word. The NMX official nodded his head in a friendly gesture and smiled the same placating yet condescending smile the colonials had probably used on Native peoples since Columbus had become the first immigrant to set foot on Native land. Jake grinned inwardly as he watched him step behind the folding tables and take a seat with the council.

As the NMX representative began his speech, Jake's eyes wandered around the room, counting every head and scanning every face. He expected Elias Dayton wouldn't be too far away from his NMX benefactor. It only took him a little more than a few minutes to spot Dayton since the hall had become a packed house and people were filling space anywhere they could. Tucked away to the left of the folding tables, nestled comfortably between two of his security enforcers, like a hotdog in a bun, stood Elias Dayton. His smug face showed nothing but what Jake could only assume was contempt for being in this poverty-stricken place with all these heathen people that couldn't matter less to him.

As the man from NMX ended his opening speech, Jake moved toward Dayton, stopping periodically to recognize a concerned chapter member and speak to them understandingly about whatever currently concerned them. The council speaker opened up the listening session to residents and recognized a middle-aged woman in a loose-fitting blue dress standing up in the middle of the crowd. Jake watched her make her way to the front of the hall and pick up the microphone from one of the folding tables. After making sure it was on, she began by introducing herself in Navajo, then spoke her mind.

"My house sits on the main road, the only way in or out of the drilling sites in my area," she began. "It used to be a quiet and peaceful place, now it's just filled with noise. Noise that wasn't there before." She adjusted the glasses on her chubby face and went on. "These trucks of yours, they create so much dust and contribute to the noise. I sat in front of my house one afternoon and counted at least eleven of them roaring up and down the road in less than thirty minutes. Not to mention some of my neighbors have your black snakes—your pipelines— running across their driveways and along the roads near them."

The crowd showed their agreement with a collective disgruntled murmur.

"Some of those roads were here long before you got here. They're school bus routes, and there are children waiting for the buses at the sides of these roads. Your drivers need to show respect for our children and drive more carefully." She paused to adjust her glasses again. "Your people, it's true, have paid us for the use of our land, but what have we suffered? We live with the drilling and the pumping and your compressors making noise all the time. They are always humming. They never stop!"

Another collective groan echoed throughout the hall as Jake continued to slowly advance through the standing crowd in the direction of Elias Dayton.

"Maybe you should come out and live with us to see how your equipment is affecting our lives." She looked at the man from NMX, but he didn't respond. All he did was stare at her. "I'm finished now. Someone else can speak."

She laid the microphone down and returned to her seat. Just as quickly a man stood up and took her place. Jake noticed that Dayton had become aware of him moving closer and took note of it as he watched the new disgruntled citizen. It felt good seeing someone else get the brunt of complaints for a change, Jake thought to himself, since it was usually him who was always on the receiving end. He continued to move casually in Dayton's direction. Jake saw him momentarily list to the right and whisper something into one henchman's ear. He smiled as he saw the henchman glare at him.

The middle-aged man stood before the assembled crowd in

a brown shirt, jeans, and cowboy boots, and seemed to hold the microphone with purpose. "Some of us here are not allotees," he said. "You have to remember that. And we live with the noise and the dust and the trouble your men cause too. What is in it for those of us who don't receive any money? The drilling on BLM land and state lands we cannot control, but what happens to the money given for the wells on Indian lands? What do we see of it? Nothing!"

The crowd became more enthused. The NMX man raised his hand and spoke confidently into the perched microphone sitting on the table in front of him like a metal bird. "So far NMX has paid out over thirty-six million dollars in royalties for our wells in the San Juan Basin on federal, state, and Indian lands." He turned his attention to the council members who were hanging on his every word. "Twenty-two million in severance and taxes, and almost eleven million to private landowners." He turned his attention back to the man speaking. "I don't know how the tribe disperses its money; that's something you all need to take up with them." He tugged absently at his tie. "And our employees on these sites have a strict code of conduct to adhere to; rest assured that we will terminate anyone who does not follow company policy. And as far as the noise— this is not an eight-to-five job. It doesn't stop just because the clock dictates or the sun goes down."

Suddenly, a large man in the second row wearing a loose red shirt wrapped by a silver concha belt stood up and shouted, "You people have crude oil storage tanks clustered together all over our land! What if there's another explosion like there was a few years ago? You guys were fracking and six wells went up! There was a huge fireball in the night sky—I could see it from my backyard!"

The crowd was becoming even more galvanized, and the

environmental activists began chanting like rhythmic druids with rhyming phrases of resistance.

"That shit burned for over three days! Oh, sure, you blamed it on some equipment malfunction, but what was the *real* reason? I think we all have a right to know!"

Jake slid up next to Elias Dayton with his arms crossed and leaned his head in close to Dayton's right shoulder. "Looks like your boss is gonna be up shit's creek tonight."

Dayton didn't respond. He just kept scanning the crowd. Jake's eyes did the same.

"You expecting trouble?" Jake asked.

Dayton snorted a laugh. "Not with these people. And not with you here." His eyes shifted to Bilagody. "But you can't be too careful these days. Someone may have a few eggs in their pockets, just waiting for their moment to heave them."

The Navajo council speaker called the man to order. He sat down unimpressed and unsatisfied.

"Sure, people who lease their land have benefited from it," the next man who took up the microphone stated. He was an elder wearing a flat, wide-brimmed cowboy hat with a silver hat band, a rhubarb-colored shirt covered in a small mass of turquoise necklaces and anchored by a matching concha belt above his worn jeans and boots. "Someone I know used that money to help put their daughter through school. And there were others that were able to send their sons to college. But all of that—all of that—does not outweigh the safety risks we suffer as a community. I think the Nation should address these public health issues for us. That's why we voted them in. They are supposed to be looking out for us. Fracking is not good for the land, no matter what you people tell us. The chemicals you use are poisoning the earth and water table during your time here, and long after you have taken all you can from us and seal these wells up with your poison trapped inside, it will *still* be here poisoning us!"

"Look, you all are welcome to take a tour of our fracking sites whenever you wish," the NMX man said. "I'll even allow you to take water samples, if you like—"

"And what good will that do?" another woman who needed no microphone stood and shouted. "I don't know about the rest of you, but I didn't understand the effects their needles would have on our families and our land." Her voice rose an octave when she spoke, and everyone could hear her clearly when she said, "Yes, I get money from these oil people. Hell, my grandma does too! And it feels good to have it! But we were never warned that the drilling was going to cause health problems and damage our water!"

The entire crowd was on its collective feet now. The activists began waving their signs and chanting their resistance more forcefully. The Navajo council speaker hammered his gavel and ordered them to be quiet. They reluctantly did.

"You people have drilled more than a hundred wells," the woman went on, "in the last three years, and during that time a number of our children have been diagnosed with cancer! What do you say to that?"

Just then, the large man from the second row rose up again and charged the tables. Elias Dayton sprang into action. He moved quickly from the wall, ran what looked to Jake to be about twenty feet of distance between them, and lunged for the man with both arms outstretched. Jake followed quickly behind. The two mountains of muscle Dayton had brought followed Jake.

The shot came quickly and silently due to the throng of chaos and the escalating noise filling the hall. Jake saw the blood explode from Elias Dayton's back and watched as all of his forward momentum was instantly misdirected from the impact of the round as his body fell into the charging man's legs, bringing him to the floor hard along with the weight of Dayton's lifeless body.

Jake looked up briefly to see that the folding tables had emptied and Dayton's hired muscle was quickly leading the NMX man to a safe place. The rest of the council had already escaped behind the imagined safety of the faux-stone dais. Jake's eyes instinctively moved to where all the people had been standing near the exits. He could see that most of them who could had decided to immediately hit the floor, while others had exited the building and could be seen running off into the failing light of day as the doors slowly closed behind them.

As Jake reached Dayton, he touched his fingers to his neck, feeling for a pulse. Finding none, he radioed in while he glanced at each of the windows at the back of the hall. When dispatch answered, he barked his commands as his eyes settled on a window with a spiderwebbed pane of glass in the lower center.

A .338, was Jake's first thought. It had to be. John Sykes had just taken Dayton out with a single shot from somewhere outside the chapter house from God knows where. That detail alone was enough to keep his brain busy telling him to stay put inside the hall until the other units arrived and provided backup. But the question now twisting through his mind as he watched the floor turn a deep shade of red was *why?* What could have soured between the two men that made Sykes take such drastic action? One didn't normally kill the golden goose.

Jake sat on the floor watching Elias Dayton bleed out across the vinyl tile. It always amazed him how much blood the human body could hold. A mere one and a half gallons, but when you watched it progressively spread out on a hard surface it always seemed like much, much more.

It was far beyond Dayton's caring now, Jake realized, that

they had traced the tracking device attached to Arthur's Bronco to the vendor, to the retail supplier, right to Dayton's front door. The next thing he would have to do is have a talk with Mr. NMX and see if he or anyone connected with the company knew about Dayton's actions or if anyone had sanctioned them. However, he also knew he was sure to hit a stone wall with that. NMX would clam up tight and politely refer any and all questions to their firm of highly paid lawyers.

And then there was the fact about Margaret's land. Was it actually in play, or had he and Arthur been wrong about its significance? When he had shared his information with the feds, they had agreed because what else could have been the motive to have the two boys killed? Somehow, Margaret's land had become the prize people were dying for—her two sons, and now Dayton, were proof of that.

It was a good thing Jake had done some digging after he made sure Margaret had a comfortable place to sleep it off. He had let his fingers do the walking though screens of computer files and discovered that due to illness, war, violence, and acts of fate, Margaret was now the only leaf left clinging to her proverbial family tree. And if NMX, or Dayton for that matter, had known that little fact they could have tried to pressure her into leasing. And if that didn't work, scare her into selling. Jake pondered that thought for a moment, then got to his feet and stepped away from the expanding pool of blood. It didn't matter what Margaret knew now. All that mattered was locating Sykes before he killed anyone else.

CHAPTER SEVENTEEN

"Dayton's dead." Jake's voice boomed through the JBL speakers of the banana on wheels.

"What!" Arthur exclaimed. "When?"

"About an hour ago. He took a bullet in the back at the Angel Peak chapter house meeting."

"I'll be damned!"

"Looks like your boy Sykes is taking care of loose ends."

"C'mon, Jake, if John was working for Dayton, why would he kill him?"

"Maybe whatever deal they had turned to shit. Wouldn't be the first time that kind of thing happened. Maybe Dayton pushed him too far by telling him to kill you."

"And when Dayton found out that John didn't kill me, he did something stupid to push him over the edge."

"That's what I'm thinking."

Arthur exhaled. "John had an ex-wife and a son—maybe Dayton threatened them."

"Then it was a pretty costly move." Arthur heard someone ask Jake something in the background and heard the big man quickly give his approval. "You find anything at the trailer? The feds should be there by now with my liaison officer."

"I found some numbers stashed in a book," Arthur said. "Long story short, I dropped Sharon at home, grabbed my hunting GPS, and right now I'm heading out to see where they take me. The numbers turned out to be coordinates."

"Be very careful," Jake said. "I'd offer go with you, but I'm going to be tied up here for a while." The line went still for a moment. "You know, if the feds find him before you do, he'll force whatever kind of outcome he wants."

The tightness Arthur felt in his chest was like someone squeezing his heart with an iron fist. The thought of Sykes forcing the issue with a suicide-by-cop scenario, or worse—execution by commanding officer—was something he knew he had to stop from happening.

"I knew something was up with him at the wake," Arthur confided. "I felt it in my gut. And you know what? No matter who finds him first, the outcome will *always* be up to him."

Jake paused. "I've got Margaret back at the station. One of my officers picked her up on a DUI."

"Jesus …"

"Don't worry," Jake reassured him. "I took care of her. She's resting and sleeping it off. She doesn't need anything more on top of what she's already been through." Jake responded to another question from the background noise again. "I had her car towed to the station and was going to have a talk with her in the morning when she sobered up, but I guess there'll be no need for that since my suspect is layin' here dead."

"Thanks, Jake."

"Don't mention it. I just couldn't see causing her any more pain." The line went silent again for a few seconds. "How close are you to where you are going?"

"Just left Aztec on Navajo Dam Road, heading southeast of Aztec Ditch. I'm probably about twenty miles out."

"That's right in the middle of some gas wells," the Navajo cop warned. "Nothing but dirt roads, cold nights, coyotes, and knocking compressors."

"Did you ever stop to think," Arthur said, "that when the Europeans came over here all they tried to do was kill us off. And when they discovered they couldn't do that, they imprisoned our leaders and stuck what was left of us on what was left of our land that they stole, so that a hundred years later they could come back and try to finish the job by poisoning our water with these wells?"

"The politicians refer to those wells and pipelines as 'critical infrastructure,'" Jake acknowledged. "Just be careful out there. If you go near some of those sites, it's considered a felony. Not to mention what a stray bullet might do."

Arthur followed Navajo Dam Road to where it veered off to the east just north of Tiger Park and the baseball field across from Tiger Pond. "I'll be fine. And when is safe drinking water going to be considered critical infrastructure? Why isn't it a felony to poison the air or the land or the water?"

"If you're asking Jake Bilagody, duly sworn officer of the Navajo Division of Public Safety, that's above my pay grade. If you're asking Jake Bilagody, respected elder of the Bitter Water clan, until we have someone like us in government, those things will never be discussed, and legislation will never be written."

"The government would never let it happen," Arthur said, continuing on the asphalt two-lane past the Kart Kanyon Speedway. The sun was now sharing the sky with the moon as it began its downward slide toward the horizon. Arthur had been counting the wells as he passed them in the high desert east of Aztec. He had noticed three already in the span of only a few miles, stationed just off the road and painted to match their surroundings so as not to be an eyesore. "At least there are a couple of Native women in Congress now. That's a first. But thanks for the heads-up," he said. "If you hear from me after this, well, it means I'm not dead."

He thumbed the big red button at the bottom of the screen and slid the phone back into the lined denim jacket that now hid his two Glock 19Cs, one cradled in the shoulder sling under his left arm and the other clipped to his right hip in the tactical holster. The bucket seat of the banana on wheels wasn't so comfortable with the addition of the Compact Colt Mustang .380 tucked into the small of his back. Each Glock carried fifteen rounds, the Colt only seven. But that was a fact Arthur knew didn't really matter in the long run. What counted was accuracy—always accuracy. As the banana's headlights turned themselves on to navigate the road before him in the twilight, the thought occurred to him that this could all be a waste of time and would prove to be nothing more than a small box canyon John Sykes had visited somewhere in the past. But he was counting on it being something more. He had no way of knowing how old the scrap of paper he had found was, but nevertheless, it was something that he had to check out.

As he topped the short rise by a telephone pole, the string of fat round bushes on his left did nothing to mitigate the roar of racing engines that reverberated from the clay oval track of the speedway. He glanced over at the lights and heard the announcer's voice calling the race with an overzealous anxiety that echoed in the evening air. Farther past the track, in a sunken area surrounded by a tall chain-link fence and excavated earth, was another well, its olive drab piping and storage tank surrounded by a protective gravel retaining berm. He shook his head and wondered why it had taken him so long to notice these intrusions before. Had he grown jaded and indifferent as he crept closer toward middle age? Why had these things not mattered to him like they did to others? That was a question that he needed to answer. But now was not the time.

He continued past the vacant Aztec Motocross track and headed toward the weathered butte ahead, noting that every graded exit he saw departing the roadway led to another well. The sweet smell of sage that filled the evening air helped his mind to run calmly and logically though the many scenarios that might play out once he located Sykes. Given John's state of mind, if there was a way to get through to him, he would try to take it. But if there was no way of reasoning with him, he would be facing the inevitable choice he didn't want to have to make. If John forced him, then he knew what he would have to do. But that was a thought he chose not to dwell on. John Sykes had been a member of *his* team. He was a brother, as close, or in some ways closer, than any brother of flesh and blood could have been. And if there was a chance to somehow reach through whatever cloud had fogged his mind and pull him back into reality, Arthur knew he had to try it. Because if he couldn't, he would be attending yet another wake.

CHAPTER EIGHTEEN

Moonlight soaked the box canyon in a cool pale light as Arthur walked away from the yellow Toyota. He had managed to find refuge for it behind a cluster of trees where it couldn't easily be seen, though the white top and yellow body seemed to attract the moon's reflected mixture of sunlight, starlight, and earthlight like a glow-in-the-dark football.

Not being familiar with the terrain of the canyon, Arthur stepped cautiously and purposefully as he moved quietly through the chilled night. Being sure to keep his breathing steady and relaxed, he held the Glock 19C from his shoulder sling comfortably in his right hand while feeling the recognizable weight of the other pistol resting on his right hip. Somewhere off in the distance a band of coyotes barked and howled, the trickster letting anyone and anything know they were there, lurking in the half-lit darkness. Arthur's ears battled against the droning noise of well compressors, their collective chorus of mechanical harmony challenging his senses to detect any out-of-place noise. As he picked his way through the shadowy canyon, a dozen fragrances filled his nostrils, and he swore he could taste each one of them on his tongue. Was his apprehension from stalking John Sykes playing that much havoc with his senses? What if Sykes had already noticed him in the night? His night-vision scope could certainly have located him picking his way up the canyon. Arthur took a deep breath and moved even more cautiously, his eyes straining against the moonlight and the uneasiness in his head.

The only thing Arthur knew for sure was that he wouldn't even hear the fatal shot, things would just simply turn black, and he would drift off into a dark world all his own to begin his journey to the next. At least the thought of Sharon not having to burn the house down (a Navajo death ritual) because he hadn't died inside of it was comforting. He had put a lot of work and time into that house to turn it from his to theirs, and he was glad that she would still be able to call it home.

A hundred yards in, the craggy canyon broke to the right and Arthur could smell something other than the perfumes of the high desert. The slight acrid scent of smoke passed over his olfactory nerves and collected in his throat. John had lit a fire. Arthur thought that an odd behavior for a man on the run because a flame would surely lead someone to him, and he wouldn't want to do that. Although it was an aroma that smelled good. It brought back memories of the times he and Sharon had gone camping in the Black Hills of South Dakota. They had pitched their cabin tent at a campsite, inflated the double high queen-sized air mattress—Sharon's choice, not his—and laid the Cosmic blue sleeping bag built for two on top of its bloated surface. Sharon had set up their small collapsible table at the other end of the tent, and on it she'd placed a small propane-powered, two-burner camp stove, a blue enamel coffeepot, and all the other items she needed to bring their home with them on the trail. That was the last time she had been truly happy, he remembered, before everything had changed. A month later, the ordeal of Leonard Kanesewah would take place, and their entire life would spiral out of control.

The farther Arthur moved into the canyon, the more the symphony of compressors gave way to the sound of night crickets and the breeze that seemed trapped between the canyon walls. That, coupled with his soft footfalls, seemed to calm him as he moved toward the smell of rising and drifting smoke. The choir of coyotes continued to bark, cry, and howl at the full, round moon as if to give it company, its blotchy glowing surface staring back at them and saying nothing in return. Arthur began to notice the sandy and rocky brush-covered canyon floor was beginning to be lined with sporadic sections of volcanic rock that seemed to spread from black canyon wall to black canyon wall. This was not simply a box canyon, Arthur realized, but a subterranean canyon carved out by an ancient lava flow that had plowed its way through the landscape long before the oceans that had covered this part of New Mexico had receded.

He looked up toward a cluster of cottonwoods standing tall on what was left of the firm ground above the arched cave where the smoke was emanating. Moving closer, he began to make out the dancing flames and the large figure squatting next to it for warmth. The night had been turning colder, colder than normal, and Arthur's lined denim jacket was having trouble fending off the chill that made the temperature feel like the middle forties instead of the ten degrees higher it should have been at this time of year.

Arthur was careful now not to make any sound that might telegraph of his approach. The closer he moved, the clearer his line of sight became. John Sykes was squatting in a thin, ribbed, new age jacket that made him look like a thinner but muscular version of the Michelin Man. Sykes lifted a cup to his mouth, then, as Arthur remembered him doing numerous times in the combat zone, pulled something from inside his jacket, unscrewed it, and slid a cigar into his open palm. After biting off the end, he used something to coax the fire from the pit and light the tip. After a few deep, satisfying inhales, Sykes blew smoke out over the fire with a relaxing *whoosh*.

Arthur stepped closer, keeping a watchful eye on John Sykes, and understanding this was going to be all about the element of surprise. He felt his heart pounding like a large powwow drum and his throat turning as rough as a dry wash in the middle of sweltering August. He knew before he had even made the drive out to the coordinates that he didn't want things to end in a way that would haunt him for the rest of his life, along with the rest of the ghosts from his past; he wanted it to end in a way that would bring his brother the help he so desperately needed. But then there were Margaret's boys to consider— Tsela and Tahoma. What justice would they receive knowing that their killer had faced no consequences at the hands of their adopted uncle or in a court of law? For that matter, how would Margaret react, knowing that her sons had not been avenged? Arthur took a deep breath and flexed his right hand around the Glock, then stood quickly.

Arthur shouted, "Don't move, John!"

Sykes remained squatted and said in a calm voice, "Didn't take long for you to get here with those coordinates I left for you."

Arthur moved forward quickly, up the gradual rocky incline, and into the yellow glow of the campfire opposite John Sykes. Sykes continued to puff on his cigar at a leisurely pace while holding a cup of what was surely alcohol from the bottle of Southern Comfort sitting on the ground by his feet.

"How did you know I'd find them?"

"I left them where a Fobbit could find them. Besides, my girl called me after you and Sharon left the house and told me you'd found them." He pulled the cigar from his lips with the fingertips of his right hand and held the smoke in his mouth, then belched it out when he added, "By the curious look on your face, I guess you didn't think she and I were still communicating."

Arthur said, "She gave the impression that you'd left her high and dry. She's a pretty good actor."

"She had to be convincing, sir," Sykes acknowledged. "I wanna tell you, I didn't kill those two boys, and I didn't take any shots at you." He lifted the bottle toward Arthur in a friendly gesture. "And I don't know who did."

Arthur declined the offering. "Open your jacket," he ordered calmly.

Sykes put the cigar back in his mouth and set the bottle back by his feet, then moved his hands slowly toward the zipper, pulled it down until it released, and carefully fanned out the flanks of the jacket. "Satisfied?"

Arthur made sure he kept the 9 mm leveled. "I found evidence you were at the scene where the boys were killed, John."

"How could there be evidence when I already told you I was never there, sir?" Sykes picked up his cup and took another drink.

"I found your fingerprints."

"Bullshit."

"Why are you lying to me, John? We have a history, man, but the evidence puts you at the scene."

"I told you that's bullshit!" Sykes stood, his eyes gleaming in the firelight, and pointed an index finger toward the ground in protest. "I was never there! Someone set me up!"

"Why?" Arthur said. "Why would anyone do that? What the hell for?"

"I don't fucking know, sir. Your guess is as good as mine. Pick a reason."

Arthur looked around. "Where's your truck and your weapons? Rosheen said you took them."

Sykes turned his head and pointed with his chin to an area down the dark canyon. "Truck's back there. You passed it on your way in. I tossed some desert camo netting over it." He moved his head again and pointed into the cave with the cottonwoods above it. "Weapons are in there. Figured I might need them if whoever is after you came after me." He pulled heavily on his cigar then tapped the ash into the popping fire. "You and me, sir, are in the same boat. We're both being fucked."

"What were you doing in Farmington the night before you came to see me in the hospital?"

"I was on my way back home from visiting my father. He lives there now."

"Where?"

"A place called the Bridges of Farmington. One of those senior living places." Sykes grinned. "Actually, that's how I heard I was being framed for the kids' murders—the guy who takes care of my dad has a son who works for the San Juan county sheriff. He told his old man, and his old man told me."

"He could lose his job over that."

"No shit. But the kid just told his old man in passing; it wasn't supposed to go any further. He knows what I'm going through with my dad and wanted to give me a heads-up."

Arthur said, "Can anyone confirm you were at the home during the time the boy's were murdered?"

"Fuck, yeah," he said. "It was Monday Night Football, so anyone sitting around us can verify I was there until I left."

"And when was that?"

"Game came on after six and finished up after ten. I—"

"This is going to be easier than I thought," a recognizable voice echoed from the darkness.

Both men turned as James Basher stepped into the light of the campfire. "You know, John, you really should be more careful about where you park that old Dodge of yours. I've had a tracker on it ever since you let us know about the lieutenant being in the hospital."

"Bash, you fucker!" Sykes growled.

"I wouldn't move, John," Basher said, stepping closer, the 9 mm in his hand able to dispose of either one of them at any given moment. "I could drop you easily from here. How 'bout you, Lieutenant? You feelin' lucky?"

Arthur stayed put. "What's your deal in this, Bash?" he said. "What did Dayton promise you? You're working for him, right?"

"A shitload of money, of course." Bash's grin gleamed in the flickering firelight. "All I had to do was kill a couple of Indians." Arthur watched as Basher's grin turned to a broad smile. "Pulling the trigger was like cumming in my pants."

Arthur felt his jaw muscles clench as his right hand tightened harder around the grip of the Glock and his left hand curled into a fist. "And me? Did you miss on purpose or just fuck up?"

Bash tilted his head comically. "I just wanted to eliminate you from the equation so that you would stay out of this. But now it looks like I'm going to have to rethink my plan." He paused. "I was going to pin it all on Sykes here and have him commit suicide to wrap it all up in a nice bundle. He was going to be just another poor soldier struggling with his own memories and stopping the pain the only way he knew how. But now I'm seeing it differently. You're going to die confronting him, and he's going to have to die by your hand." Bash stepped closer. "Why don't you be so kind as to toss your weapon over here, Lieutenant."

Arthur reluctantly tossed his Glock, heard it clamber among the rocks at Bash's feet. Carefully squatting, Bash picked it up, stood, and tucked his own 9 mm into the waistband of his pants as he trained the Glock on Arthur. "Now the other one," Bash said, grinning. "When we were in-country, you always carried two pieces." He waved the semiautomatic. "C'mon, don't disappoint me now."

Arthur pushed back the flank of his denim jacket, reached his right hand inside, and unsnapped the tactical holster. He carefully pulled out the second Glock and tossed it where he had thrown the other pistol.

Bash picked it up and turned his attention to Sykes. "Now you, John. What tricks have you got up your sleeve?"

Sykes opened his jacket again to reveal no weapon. Arthur noticed how his eyes never left Bash's. There wasn't a knife big enough, he thought, to cut the tension between them, no matter how many times they'd had each other's back in the sandbox.

"How long have you been a part of the Patriots?" Arthur asked.

Bash's boisterous laugh echoed from the cave througout the dark canyon. "I'm not a part of those fucking wannabes," he said indignantly. "After I got out of the service, I tried to re-up more than once, but they wouldn't fucking have me. Said my brain was all messed up. Well, they were the ones that messed it up! Because they turned me into a killer, and I fucking let them! They said I had traumatic brain injuries that prohibited them from re-enlistment." Bash made sure he kept one Glock trained on Arthur, while the other remained centered on Sykes. "Why aren't you the same as the rest of us? The war made you a killer too." Bash shook his head, as if to rid himself of a flurry of demons. "Sometimes, Lieutenant, I feel like I'm living on the edge of nowhere. Did you know I've spent the last eight years of my life plotting my own death? Hell, I even tried to blow my brains out the other day, but the fucking hammer fell on a dud." Bash returned his attention to Sykes.

"I can get you help, James," Arthur promised.

"Fuck you and your help!"

Arthur noticed Basher becoming agitated and a bit shaky, spurred on by the anxiety racing through him now. Sykes looked at Arthur and then back at Basher.

"How'd you get involved with the Patriots?" Arthur asked.

Keep calm, John. Just keep calm.

"Dayton hired me on his own figuring that if he could get the broad to sell her land to him, he could, in turn, lease it to NMX under a shadow company and work out a profitable deal for himself."

"Then what made you kill him?" Arthur said.

Bash's expression was curious, and the question seemed to make him focus. Arthur had Sykes' attention as well.

"You heard already, huh?" Bash snickered. "That was an unfortunate consequence. I was aiming for the NMX exec at the table. He had been stumbling closer to what Dayton was doing, so he gave me another bonus to take him out. But when some asshole stood up and headed for the panel, Dayton just got in the way." He shrugged. "Oops."

Arthur made a mental note of the smirk on Bash's face. He thought it needed to be smacked off, and hard. But he wasn't close enough to do it. And if he tried to move closer, it might force Bash to kill them both and leave them out here in this box canyon for the bobcats and cougars to feed on, leaving the coyotes to clean up the scraps. The Colt Mustang nestling snug and hard against his lower back constantly reminded him it was there, ready and willing to bark whenever he made the judgment call. Arthur looked at Sykes and slightly shook his head in a motion not telegraphed to Bash.

"Guess I'm killing two birds with one stone, you might say."

Bash's eyes shifted between both men. "I already have them

looking for our friend here, so why not add another kill to his roster. I have the rifle I used to kill the boys in my truck. It's wiped clean, and I was going to leave it among John's stash so the cops would find it and tie it to him. Dayton had already paid me up front for the two boys, but after I didn't take you out—well, he didn't care too much for that. But what was he going to do?"

"Why me, man?" Sykes said. "I saved your ass plenty of times outside the fence."

"What can I say, buddy, purely collateral damage. The side effect of war. Nothing personal." He looked at Arthur. "I'm guessing you found the gum wrapper, sir?"

Arthur nodded.

"Gum wrapper?" Sykes repeated.

"You know you really should recycle more, John. You shouldn't be tossing things like gum wrappers on the ground." Bash smiled knowingly. "The last time you took me out to that desolate pile of shit where you shoot, I picked it up and pretended to throw it out. You wouldn't want some poor creature to come along and get that paper stuck in its throat because it smelled like spearmint."

Out of the corner of his eye, just inside the farthest edge of his visual acuity, Arthur noticed Sykes' right hand slowly moving behind his back. Arthur decided to focus Bash's attention back on him. If Sykes had a play, he would have to go with it. "So no one besides that exec at NMX knew what Dayton was up to?" Arthur hoped he was buying some time. And the question seemed to give Sykes enough time to get his hand on whatever it was he had stashed behind his back.

"Nope. Dayton may have been a tool, but he was no idiot. He played his moves pretty close to the vest. It was only after the exec began sniffing around that Dayton seemed to get nervous." Bash's fingers settled firmly around the grip of

Arthur's Glocks, his index fingers resting comfortably on each of the triggers. "It's kind of apropos, don't you think?"

"What is?" Arthur said.

"Remember what the Corps chaplain always used to tell us when we were at the FOB between missions? He said that death waits in the dark for all of us." The two men watched as Bash's arms rose and leveled each of the weapons at their chests. "I guess he was right. Till Valhalla, gentlemen."

Suddenly, Bash's attention shifted to John Sykes as Sykes' big hand swung forward rapidly from behind his back. Arthur noticed something flash above the glow of the campfire and sail through the air in a horizontal path. Bash quickly read the movement and dodged the bowie knife Sykes had intended to lodge into the upper-left quadrant of his torso. Reflexively, Bash's left hand twitched, and his finger made the Glock fire once. Sykes spun around instantly and fell to the ground.

Arthur made his move without giving it a conscious thought. Quickly he reached around his back and pulled the Colt Mustang .380 from the back of his waistband. He'd already chambered a round before tucking it away, and it only took a split second for him to thumb back the hammer and release the side safety before leveling it at James Basher's chest. Instantly, Arthur heard the crack of the report and felt the lightweight pistol bucking consecutively in his hands. The muzzle flashed each of the four times in response to his finger pulling the trigger, leaving behind the smell of propellant floating in the night air.

Bash spun on impact from the four rounds hitting their target but managed to maintain his balance as he raised the 9 mm a second time. Arthur fired three more rounds, the slide kicking violently each time, forcing the weapon to buck hard again and again and again, before locking in the slide in the open position. Empty. The responding shot squeezed off by James Basher rocketed into the night sky as Arthur watched him stumble backward and topple onto the rocks behind him on the canyon floor.

Arthur thumbed the slide release of the .380 and heard it snap home. Shoving it into the waistband behind his back, he rushed to Basher, rescuing his Glocks from the dirt and rocks and holstering them both before grabbing Bash's 9 mm and tossing it out of reach. Bash's eyes were open wide but seeing nothing. They had been staring at the stars in the sky before he had succumbed to his own darkness, and it had taken hold of him. His nightmares had been finally put to rest along with his soul. In Arthur's world, the Navajo world, James Basher's spirit had already left his body with his last breath and was probably floating around them now, watching them, listening to them, cursing them. Arthur felt a chill move through him, and he shivered rigidly. It was a chill far colder than the air of a desert night and it made him uneasy. Arthur used the fingers of his right hand to close Basher's eyes before checking on Sykes.

"How badly are you hit?" Arthur said. "Can you get up?"

"Bastard got me in the left shoulder," Sykes complained. "Same place I took that shrapnel from that IED." One of his big hands was gripping his shoulder and doing its best to suppress the flow of blood. "Fucker!"

"That was a stupid thing to do," Arthur chided, smiling. "But it worked."

"I figured you had a play of some kind in mind, sir." Arthur helped Sykes to his feet. "Surprised the hell outta me you had a third weapon."

"Adapt and overcome, brother," Arthur said.

Sykes just smiled. "Oo-rah!"

"Let's get you to a hospital."

As the two men stumbled past the campfire, they paused briefly in order for Arthur to kick enough dirt on it to extinguish it. They had moved about twenty more paces when Sykes stopped him, stepped over a few feet, and squatted down. Arthur saw him pick up his knife, stand, and return it to the leather sheath that hung horizontally behind his back from his belt and snapped the band on it.

"I never saw that," Arthur said.

Sykes grinned. "You never asked me to turn around."

Arthur pulled his cell phone from his jacket pocket, tapped it to life, and dialed a number.

"Jake," he said in a hurried fashion. "I've got Sykes. I'm taking him to the hospital. He's been shot."

"You shoot him?"

"It's a long story," Arthur said. "And, boy, were we both wrong."

CHAPTER NINETEEN

Two hours after admitting John Sykes into San Juan Regional Medical Center, Arthur's phone buzzed in his shirt pocket. "Where are you?" Bilagody asked.

"I'm on my way to Margaret's," Arthur said as he headed west past the illuminated facade of the Northern Edge Casino. The moon hung high and bright in the night sky, its radiant glow adding to the glare of the banana on wheels' headlights. "I wanted to tell her it was over. I wanted her to know that her boys could rest in peace."

"Uh-huh," Jake acknowledged. "By the way, your boy Sykes is going to make it through surgery. The initial exploratory showed the bullet tore up some tissue and muscle before lodging in the bone. Good news is the slug missed any major nerves or arteries. He'll be on antibiotics and have to do some rehab, but he shouldn't lose any movement of the shoulder."

The digital clock on the banana's dash said it was 11:58 p.m. "Damn," he said out loud, "I need to call Sharon. She'll be wondering what the hell's going on."

"I can remember those days," Jake remarked, a melancholy twinge to his voice. "Many years ago."

"Speaking of that," Arthur prodded, "I've been meaning to ask how you're doing?"

Jake took a deep breath and exhaled. "Good, I guess. I'm good. It's just sometimes I get thinking about things I shouldn't be thinking about. Drags me down."

"Have you spoken with Nizhoni?"

"No," Jake said. "And she hasn't bothered to contact me either. What would be the sense of it anyway? It's over. It's done." He exhaled again, this time deeply, with all the weight of the emptiness he felt when he allowed himself to think of her crushing him. "If nothing changes, I'm just gonna be an old man with no one around to give a damn."

Arthur smiled. "You've got me."

"As gratifying as that sounds, it's not quite the same, my friend."

Arthur paused, unsure of how to continue, then brought the conversation back to the present. "You uncover anything more about this mess yet?"

"Mr. Sonori," Jake explained, "the NMX executive at the chapter house meeting, was very forthcoming with me. It seems he had been contacted by one of his company's drilling foremen who told him that the superintendent had been funneling money from the company accounts into the coffers of Patriot security, seemingly for security work that was later discovered to be falsified."

"He was the target that night, you know," Arthur said. "Basher said Dayton just got in the way."

"That's what Mr. Sonori thought," Jake said. "His guess was that the superintendent told Dayton he'd been discovered, and that's why Sonori figured it was just a matter of time before the whole thing escalated, and he'd move to the top of the list. Apparently, this whole thing started when Dayton got wind of the murder of Joseph Benally—that's the man who was beaten up and tossed in Antelope canyon. He threatened to expose the workers, which, in turn, led the foreman to contact the superintendent who was more than willing to do whatever it took to shove it under the rug to cover his ass with the company. No press is good press, so to speak."

"So Dayton was blackmailing him, and he was paying?"

"Every month. Only thing is," Jake added, "they didn't figure on the foreman's conscience getting the better of him. He cracked under the pressure and went through a back channel to get hold of Sonori."

Arthur saw the sign for Upper Fruitland come and go and watched the moonlight play against the cliffs to his left.

"I'm going to need a statement from you," Jake said, "about what happened and why back in that canyon. Agent Thorne is pushing me to haul your ass in. I told him I didn't know where you were."

Arthur passed over the top of Upper Fruitland Tunnel and headed up the guardrail-lined incline. The lanes had been split into three now, and he stayed in the fast lane and moved with it with high beams reaching out in front of him. He rattled off what James Basher had told him in the canyon about Dayton making a play for Margaret's forty acres. "Dayton was running a game either way," Arthur said. "He was using blackmail to strip more money from NMX, while using the murder to rob Margaret of her boys so she would have nothing left to lose if she sold the land to him. Look, I've gotta go. I'll tell you more after I see Margret." He ended the call and shoved the phone back into his shirt pocket.

Just after cresting the hill, Arthur noticed the small power station off to his right and the white sign announcing the direction of Ojo Amarillo Elementary School. He slowed and turned left onto N3035. Soon the short white walls of the Navajo housing development rose in elevated increments to the entrance. He tapped the brakes and swung the Toyota through the entrance.

It was heartbreaking, Arthur reflected as he drove through the sparsely lit streets, that his people were living in such conditions. The Navajo Housing Authority was created to build affordable housing for its people, but all they had proved to be able to do was waste the funds they have been given. He remembered Sharon doing a report on how over the last ten years the NHA had received over eight hundred million dollars of federal funding and had only constructed eleven hundred homes, all while his people continued to live in previously built homes in need of renovating and full of overcrowded conditions, while still others had to find shelter in storage units throughout the reservation.

It was true, he acknowledged, that the level of financial incompetency, mismanagement, and fraud, coupled with the many construction delays that were rampant throughout the reservation's twenty-seven thousand square miles, had brought the NHA's fifty-five-year history to a tipping point. He shook his head and raked his fingers through his hair as he passed the abandoned and disheveled homes mixed among the occupied and neat homes. Maybe Margaret *should* sell her land, he thought, take the money and just get out. Or at the very least, agree to lease the land and reap some kind of benefit from doing so. He would have to talk to her about that. If she was awake and sober. If she was awake and drunk, he would still tell her that her sons' murders had been solved. But Arthur sensed, even with that news, there was no absolution in this for him. He had failed the boys. He had failed their father. And, even worse, he had failed Margaret.

As Arthur turned the corner, he saw Margaret's Dodge

Diplomat parked on the concrete driveway underneath the carport. He noticed lights were on in the house and was at least glad that Jake had been as kind as he had been to her. He pulled the Toyota onto the concrete pad behind her car, turned off the engine, and sat for a moment, his mind drifting back to those teenage days when everything in life had seemed possible when they were both so young with the whole world ahead of them. He gathered in a deep breath and let it out, then got out and walked up to her front door. Knocking three times, he waited.

Nothing.

He knocked again.

More nothing.

His finger pushed the lighted doorbell, but there was no sound that followed the motion. He formed a fist and pounded three more times on the door. "Margaret!"

Still nothing but resounding quiet.

He looked to the left and right and back to the left again. His heart jumped in his chest and seemed to tighten, his legs moved quickly to the front windows, but the curtains were drawn, and his view of the inside was obstructed. Running between the vehicles, he trotted around to the rear of the house and looked through the kitchen window between the partially drawn curtains. His view was obstructed by the table they had sat at together only a few days ago, but he could make out her still figure on the floor, the chair she had been sitting on hastily pushed askew as if she had fallen. There was an almost-empty bottle of Honey Jack sitting on the table with a tipped-over glass lying next to it.

"Margaret!" he yelled again desperately, then ran back to the front door as quickly as his aching legs could take him. Without thinking, he tried ramming the door with his shoulder by putting all the weight and strength he could muster behind it. Pain coursed through his arm and right side and his left hand massaged his shoulder. Regrouping his thoughts, he kicked the door by the lock, his pulsating thigh muscles coiling like a kickboxer's ratcheting up for the final knockout blow. To his amazement, the door held. He conjured up even more strength and kicked again. The door pushed in slightly as the jamb began to split. He summoned up a strength he hadn't employed since he kicked in doors in Iraq and slammed his foot hard into the door, forcing it to break free and swing open violently, burying the doorknob in the drywall behind it.

"Margaret!" Arthur called out again, hurtling himself through the living room, then the hallway, past the bedrooms, and into the small kitchen. Dropping to his knees beside her, his fingers searched intently for a pulse, but located only a faint murmur of life through the soft skin of her throat. Pulling his phone from his pocket, he dialed 911. Suddenly, out of the corner of his eye, he caught sight of what the table and her body had hidden. An amber plastic bottle lay on the floor, its white cap close by. Arthur rolled the bottle into view. The label read, *Lorazepam 2 mg, Qty 30.* Filled only yesterday. And all thirty were missing.

The operator answered, "911, what is your emergency?"

Arthur rattled off the address and what he had found.

"I need someone here *now!*" he added before tossing his phone onto the kitchen table. The disembodied voice of the operator continued to squawk from the table as Arthur's fingers searched again for the fading pulse. As he sat in the loud silence of the kitchen, he felt her life slowly slip away with each faint throb of her jugular … until the diminishing rhythm of her body's dance faded completely.

Arthur sat on the floor, his legs twisted beneath him and his body shivering with every ounce of life in him that was urging him not to cry, for crying and other demonstrations of grief were not to be shown so that the spirit of the deceased could travel to the next world without interruption. But he couldn't stop his lower lip from trembling and his face from contorting and growing wet with a flow of tears that ran down in anguish as his heart painfully beat in his chest with a sorrow that he fought back with every inch of his being. He reached out a hand carefully and gently brushed away some strands of hair that had fallen over her face—that sweet face, that affectionate face that had been floating through his memory ever since that day at Flat Iron Rock. Sharon had seen it. She had known it. But she never questioned it because a woman's intuition always knew the difference between a fond memory and something more.

And then there were her eyes. Eyes that now appeared lifeless and yet seemed to have that wonder, that revelation of the *what next* that only the dying have the privilege of under-standing. Arthur moved his legs from underneath himself and stretched them out before him. He laid her head gently upon his lap and closed her eyes like they do in films. His will had become the dam that had finally held his emotions in check. All for her. So that she might have a safe and mean-ingful journey. This death was so very different than that of James Basher that he had only just witnessed and taken part in. Arthur wondered if Margaret's spirit was lingering, hold-ing on for just one more minute with him, one more delicate second that would give them both solace.

After all, death was not the end of life but the beginning of the afterlife. It was a sacred part of the traditional Navajo belief system that birth and life and death are all part of an ongoing cycle. A cycle that is not to be feared but to be accepted as the progression of all things. The body was a blessed vessel. And Arthur gave no thought to fearing her death. He did not fear that her spirit would return to the land of the living and manifest itself in ways spoken of by the old ones. He did not fear any *Chindi*. For there was no evil in this woman. She would never hurt him. He had known that from the very day they had lain together in the tall grasses by the wash. He knew then that only good was to come from this woman. And all these years later only good *had* come from her. He was sure of it.

CHAPTER TWENTY

Arthur and Sharon sat together on the couch in Janet Peterson's office in Santa Fe. It was the first week of September and the blistering days of August were over for another year. The low hundreds had been replaced by the mideighties and would soon be plummeting to the midforties by December. They were holding hands and smiling perfunctorily as Dr. Peterson brought Arthur up to speed on Sharon's first session. There were two glasses of water on the coffee table in front of them on sandstone coasters, Kokopelli dancing on Sharon's and the Zia symbol decorating Arthur's. The short, fanned-out pile of *Psychology Today* magazines puzzled him. They looked askew. They looked as though someone had removed one and left a gap by not putting it back where it belonged.

It had been a few weeks since he had found Margaret on the floor of her kitchen. The thought of it was still fresh in his mind. Just one more ghost he would have to reconcile into a tiny box in his brain that would make it harder to haunt him in the days and weeks and years to come. But that was why he was here today, to find a way to open up all those hundreds of boxes he kept neatly stacked and organized and labeled and dated in his brain and let the ghosts he thought he had sealed up inside them out again to run free throughout the maze of his memory.

"I'm so glad you decided to join us today, Mr. Nakai," Janet Peterson said. Her pantsuit was a shade of gray Arthur had not seen before and didn't care to witness again. "I think it's always best when couples that have gone through traumas such as yours, that you both can let go of any preconceived notions and speak freely and openly about whatever it is you're feeling and what is affecting you both individually and collectively." Janet Peterson gave them a conciliatory smile. "Shall we begin?"

ACKNOWLEDGMENTS

The locations chosen for this novel center around the northern New Mexico towns on and around the Navajo Reservation of Nenahnezad, Kirtland, and Upper and Lower Fruitland, as well as the sixty-five-million-year-old formations of the Angel Peak Badlands and the towering rock of the Kirtland Formation from the late cretaceous period known as Flat Iron Rock. While many of the locations in this novel actually exist, a few are fictitious out of necessity. I would like to thank my friends Bettina Costagno, Bobby Mason, and Arnold Clifford—the encyclopedia of the Four Corners and well-known botanist and geologist who I was fortunate to meet—for breathing life into the area that I love so much and telling me of its rich history. Arnold, I hope to learn a great deal more from you in the future. I also wish to thank Maria Rose Biye, Lydia Fasthorse, Rochelle MacArthur, and Delane Atcitty for sharing their knowledge with me. As always, I would like to thank my agent, Richard Curtis, for his constant support and friendship and my editor, Peggy Hageman, for her nurturing guidance.